AN ENDLESS KIND OF LOVE

KRISTA LAKES

ZIRCONIA PUBLISHING, INC.

ABOUT THIS BOOK

"I thought you were beautiful the first time I saw you in the rain..."

Dylan:

The sudden death of Dylan's father was a wake-up call.

After pouring a decade of his life into his company, Dylan felt like had nothing to show for it. No wife, no kids, no family. With no destination in mind, he sells his company and wanders the world, eventually finding himself in Silver Springs...

Bonnie:

Bonnie Kincaid is also on the run... for her life. The police can't keep her safe. Things look hopeless when her car breaks down in the remote mountains of Colorado. A handsome man rescues her, fixes her car, but also gives her a reason to stop running. For the first time in a long time, she feels safe.

Unfortunately, both Bonnie and Dylan's pasts catch up with them, and in order to put down roots to grow a family, they have to stop running.

But **they** aren't finished with her yet...

To my ARC readers who are amazing. I couldn't write these books without fantastic readers like you!

Chapter 1

"DAMN YOU DIRTY rotten piece of metal!"

The words that continued to come out of Bonnie Kincaid's mouth would have made her mother blush. If her mother had been there, she would have washed her daughter's mouth out with soap, even though Bonnie was twenty-seven years old.

Bonnie cursed once more at her car engine and kicked the front fender hard enough to make her wince. The damn car was dead on the side of a lonely country road in the middle of God-knew-where of the Colorado mountains. Bonnie's AAA membership had run out about two months ago, along with every other thing in her life.

She was stuck.

Lightning crackled around the edges of the darkening clouds. The wind whispered to the pine trees and mountain fields that rain was coming. She slammed the hood of her car down and spat out another curse before apologizing to her vehicle. She didn't want the poor car to hate her.

She sat down hard in the driver's seat with her feet on the dirt road and checked her phone. No bars. Not even the hint of reception. She stood up and walked around holding her hand up to the sky, but nothing changed. Her phone was useless up here in the mountains.

Another rumble of thunder passed overhead, and she looked up at the sky. The sun was setting behind the mountains to the west as the storm rolled in from the north. It made for a pretty picture with the sun turning the sky an ominous red and glinting off the dark clouds, but she wasn't in the mood to appreciate it.

She stuck her phone back in her pocket and ran her fingers through her hair trying to figure out what to do next. She had been stopped for at least ten minutes now and hadn't seen another car drive past the entire time. There was a very good possibility that no one would ever drive by.

"Yeah, Bonnie, take the random dirt road. It'll totally be scenic and awesome," she told herself aloud. She rolled her eyes at her own stupidity. "Yup. That was a great idea."

She glanced around, hoping against hope that someone was going to come and rescue her, even though she knew it wasn't going to happen. She was going to have to rescue herself. With a sigh, she got up, pulled the keys from the ignition, closed the car door and started walking up the road. She knew there was nothing for at least five miles behind her. She hoped that maybe something was up ahead, or at least a high spot to get better reception.

She climbed the dusty hill, feeling the increase of elevation sucking all the oxygen from her lungs. She was from a small town just outside Atlantic City, so being over a mile high was a hard adjustment. She was fairly active, but she was still gasping for breath as she came over the top of the small hill. Elevation was brutal to the body.

The only warning that Bonnie got that something was about to happen was a single clap of thunder. Immediately after, the sky opened up and dumped rain directly on top of her. It was different than the summer rain she was used to. It was ice cold and made of tiny drops that felt like needles. It soaked her thin t-shirt in seconds. The wind whipped up, moaning through the pines. She shivered and wrapped her arms around herself, trying to decide if she should keep going or head back to the car and wait the storm out.

She was about to turn around when she saw the light. It was about a mile up ahead and called out to her in the deepening darkness of the storm. Multiple windows lit up with a cheerful yellow glow against the darkness of the storm. It looked welcoming, even from far away.

Bonnie tucked her head, pushing her dark blonde hair back over her shoulder and trudging down the now-mud road toward the welcoming lights. She risked a glance at her phone and found that she still had no signal. She sighed and kept walking.

This was not how she had planned this drive to go at all. To be honest, this was not how she had planned her life to go at all either.

Her life had been simple. She had lived with her brother and had a teaching job she adored. She didn't currently have a boyfriend, but that was something she was working on.

Then, just like this storm, it had all come crashing down around her. And now, here she was, stuck on the side of the road during a trip through the mountains. Alone.

She'd been driving along one of the smaller highways and saw the winding dirt road. She had planned on taking the small back road up to the top of the mountain and seeing the sunset from the top. The map on her phone made it look like she could have gotten up there and had the view all to herself.

"I should have just taken the highway," she mumbled, wrapping her arms around her a little tighter to try and stay warm. The temperature was dropping quickly now that the sun had set. Wind from the storm whipped at her wet hair and flung raindrops into her face. She wondered if they were going to turn to snow they felt so cold.

She kept her legs moving. Step by step, she was going to make it to that house and use their phone. The thunder made her nervous, and she stayed to the side of the road.

"At least Brett's not here," she murmured to herself, stepping around a large puddle. If her little brother had been there, he would have pushed her into that puddle with a laugh. He was twenty-five but still just as annoying as when he was five years old and pulling the heads off her Barbies. While they successfully shared an apartment, it was only because they had separate rooms and completely opposite work schedules. He worked nights as security at the docks while she worked at the local elementary school as a special education teacher.

But that was over now. Her work was gone. Her life was gone. She had to keep running to stay safe. To keep her little brother safe. From *them*. It made her heart ache, and she sent a prayer up to the storming sky to watch over her little brother.

She shivered as she walked up the big wooden porch to a large building. It reminded her of the dining hall at the summer camp she'd gone to as a kid. Even the chairs tucked under the awning were the same as the ones she remembered.

There was a big wooden door, but no obvious knocker or doorbell. She chewed on her lip for a moment as she decided what to do next. She wasn't sure if she should knock or just go straight in. If it was a summer camp like she suspected, no one would be listening for a random knock. If it wasn't a camp, she would give someone a surprise.

She raised her hand to knock. Better to knock first, then try the door if no one answered. Her knuckles tingled with the cold as she rapped them against the wood. It was hard to make a fist her fingers were so frozen. Who knew the rain up in the mountains could be so cold?

She counted to ten and went to reach for the doorknob just as the big door creaked open. She was suddenly very glad she'd gone with the knocking plan.

The light shining from the door hurt her eyes after the dark of the storm. All she could make out was a large, masculine shaped blur against the sudden brightness.

"Pickup is on the other side of the ranch," a deep voice told her. "The kids aren't in this building."

The tone was kind but weary as if the man had to give this speech more often than he liked. She recognized it as the one she used herself directing parents to the pickup area across the field of her school.

"I don't have any kids here," she said quickly. Another peal of thunder echoed behind her as she wrapped her arms around her core and shivered. "My car broke down a mile or so that way. I don't have any cell service. Is there a phone I can borrow?"

She looked up at the man in front of her. The light came from behind him, but her eyes were used to it now. He was tall and well built with biceps peeking out from under his camp t-shirt. His black hair was shaggy around his ears and hung into his dark brown eyes. His jaw was strong, but there was a soft kindness to his face that she immediately liked. If he smiled, she was sure he could model in a magazine.

She wiped water from her forehead and wondered just how much like a wet rat she looked like. She was sure she didn't look pretty, which was a shame because he was an attractive man. It was just her luck a good looking guy would answer the door when she looked like something the cat dragged in.

His eyes softened as he looked her over, and he winced. She decided she must look super pathetic.

"Come on in," he said, moving to the side. "Let's get you dried off and then you can use the phone."

She sighed with relief and gratefully stepped through the door into the warm yellow light.

Chapter 2

DYLAN CAREFULLY STACKED the last of the clean dishes from the sink and set them in the cupboard. It had taken him almost an hour to get through them since the industrial dishwasher for the camp had broken down. He'd washed them all by hand so that the camp would have clean dishes for breakfast tomorrow.

It wasn't his job to do dishes. Technically, he didn't really have a true position at the camp, but he was here to help out. The owners Carter and Mia were his friends, so when he'd asked for something to do, they'd given him free range on the ranch. He fixed cars, taught classes, worked with kids, and helped out with whatever repairs the ranch needed. Today, the ranch needed a dishwasher.

He drained the sink and chuckled at his dishpan hands. Who would have thought that a billionaire would be doing dishes? It felt good though. Working at the ranch with the foster kids and actually making a difference in their lives felt better than earning money ever did. He felt lighter here. Doing dishes was better for his soul than sitting at his computer.

He went to the kitchen with a clean washcloth one last time to make sure it was ready for the morning. Chef would be pleased with his work. Thunder rumbled, and rain beat against the roof. He was glad he was inside tonight. The storm outside sounded terrible.

He almost didn't hear the knock on the kitchen door. He most certainly wasn't listening for it, but he managed to hear it over the din of the storm. He figured it was probably just a foster parent on the wrong side of the camp. It seemed like once a week someone would miss all the signs pointing to the pickup area and end up at the kitchen door.

He opened the door, ready to tell them to turn around and head back the way they came. He had no desire to fight with the locked gate at the East entrance to the ranch to let them out. They could go back the way they'd come. He pulled back the door to see a woman standing on the porch.

"Pickup is on the other side of the ranch," he said. "The kids aren't here right now."

The woman blinked slowly, as if she didn't quite get what he was saying. She was absolutely drenched. That was the first thing he noticed. The second was that she was possibly the most beautiful woman he'd ever seen. Her dark blonde hair was plastered to her head and ran down her back in silky rivulets. The thin t-shirt she had on hung to her curves like a second skin.

"I'm not a parent," she explained, looking up at him with dark brown eyes that did something to his chest. "My car broke down a couple of miles that way. I don't have any cell service out here. Is there a phone I can borrow?"

The wind howled past the pine trees, and a fresh sheet of rain fell from the sky. She shivered and wrapped her arms around herself a little tighter. There was no way he could let her go back out in that. She had to be freezing.

She needed to get warm and out of the storm. The desire to protect her warmed in his chest. He pulled the door open wider.

"Come on in," he told her, stepping off to the side.

She looked at him for a moment, as if deciding what to do. He hated that she would even think that he might hurt her, but then again, she didn't know him. She sighed and stepped into the warmth, making him smile.

He led her through the kitchen and out into the eating area where he knew Mia and Laura were discussing plans for the week. The two women would make her feel at ease, and they would know better what to do with a soaking wet woman than he would.

Mia and Laura were fast at work at one of the big tables generally used for eating. They had all sorts of papers spread out among them; their heads bent as they figured out their plans. Mia's hand reached out to rock the car-seat with her sleeping baby next to her. He still couldn't believe how big little Mirelle was getting. She had such joy and life to her that it was hard to believe she'd only been on the planet a few months.

"Dylan, are you still cleaning up?" Mia asked without looking up. "If you keep this up, we'll have to pay you or something."

Laura chuckled and turned to look at him. Her eyebrows went up as she took in the soaking wet woman behind him. "Who's this?" she asked, surprise in her voice.

"Her car broke down on No-man's Road," he explained. The woman shivered, and he wished he could wrap his arms around her and warm her up, but towels would be better. "Where do we keep the extra towels?"

"You poor thing," Mia said, hopping up from her chair and hurrying over. "Here have a seat," she told the woman, ushering her toward the table.

"I'll grab the towels," Laura said, already halfway to the storage area.

"Thank you," the woman stammered, her teeth chattering from the cold.

"Dylan, will you go grab her a cup of tea?" Mia asked. "We have some water on the stove already."

"Of course," he replied quickly, angry that he hadn't thought of it himself. As he hurried off to the kitchen, he heard them continue to talk. He saw the pot on the stove, so all he had to do was grab a mug and a teabag.

"I'm guessing you went out in the rain since your phone doesn't have reception up here," Mia said. Dylan nearly dropped the mug in his haste to get it out of the cabinet.

"I'm just glad I saw the lights of the house. I was about to turn around," the woman replied. "Where am I, by the way?"

"You're at Mountain Hope Ranch in Silver Springs," Mia replied. "We're a camp for foster kids to come learn life skills and make great memories in the process."

Dylan quickly dropped a chamomile tea bag into the cup and poured the hot water over it, scalding his hand in the process. He soldiered on, wanting to get back to their guest.

"I'm Mia Williamson. I'm the director," Mia continued in the other room. "This is Laura. She is our barn manager. Let's get you dried off."

He realized Laura must have appeared with the towels as he set the teapot of hot water back on the stove. He picked up the mug and hurried back out to the cafeteria to see the woman wrapped up in fluffy towels. She looked warmer and most certainly happier.

"And of course, you've already met Dylan, our resident handyman," Mia added motioning toward Dylan.

The woman looked over and smiled at him as he set her tea down on the table in front of her. Now that she was warm, her smile was softer and less forced. It made his heart flutter. If just a small smile could do that to him, he wasn't sure what would happen if she really smiled at him. He was fairly sure he'd die of a heart attack.

He smiled back and took a seat off to the side. He didn't want to intimidate her. She'd already had a rough night, but he did want to hear her story. He found himself wanting to know everything about her. Thunder rumbled outside, and he had to wonder what he'd brought into his life with this storm.

Chapter 3

onnie

FOR THE FIRST time in weeks, Bonnie felt safe. She had a fluffy towel draped over her shoulders with another wrapped around her body and a third drying her hair. She sipped gingerly at the hot chamomile tea in her hands. A small sigh of relief rippled through her.

The knot of tension that seemed to live in between her shoulder blades relaxed just a little bit. She wasn't shivering anymore, and she wasn't afraid. It almost felt like a dream after the past few weeks.

"So, what were you doing out on No-man's Road?" Laura asked, drinking from her cup of tea. "It's kind of off the beaten path."

She and Mia sat across from her at the large square table, and Dylan had pulled up a chair catty-corner to them. Bonnie was doing her best not to look at him too much. She had a bad habit of staring at handsome men.

"I was trying to enjoy the mountains," Bonnie explained. "I thought my car could handle it since it didn't look too steep. Apparently not."

Laura nodded. "Are you from around here? Or just driving through?"

"Um, just passing through," Bonnie replied. She adjusted the towel over her shoulders.

"Where are you headed?" Laura pressed. Her voice was friendly, but the tension in Bonnie's shoulders started to creep up again.

"Laura, stop interrogating the poor woman," Mia said gently, setting her tea on the table. "If she doesn't want to tell us, she doesn't have to."

"Thank you," Bonnie replied quietly, looking into her own cup of tea. She looked up at the faces of the people around her. They were kind. It gave her courage. "Actually, I'm kind of on the run."

"From what?" Laura asked, leaning forward with excitement in her eyes. Mia gave her a stern look that Laura completely ignored.

"My ex. It's a bad situation, and I needed to get away from him," Bonnie lied. It was her standard go-to lie now, but she couldn't talk about *them*. Her most recent ex-boyfriend was happily married and living in Reno. He wouldn't appreciate being used like this, but it was better this way. She hated lying to these people who were helping her but, no one asked questions about why she was running from an ex. No one asked her to prove it or said she was making things up. It was far more believable than the truth.

"That's terrible," Laura whispered, her green eyes wide. Mia nodded as well.

"I was taking the back road because it not only looked prettier, but I'm trying to stay away from busy places. I don't really feel safe in crowds right now," Bonnie explained with a shrug. She happened to look over at Dylan to see his brow darken. He looked over at the door like he was expecting her ex to walk through it at any moment and he was going to beat the shit out of the guy.

"He won't find you here," Dylan assured her, his deep brown eyes meeting hers. She believed him. The knot in her shoulders relaxed a little more.

"Anyway, that's why I was out there," she finished lamely, forcing herself to look away from him. "I was looking for scenic views and once again chose poorly."

"That's terrible," Laura said, shaking her head. She paused and frowned. "I just realized that we didn't get your name."

"Oh! I'm Bonnie." She smiled at the two women and Dylan. "Bonnie Kincaid. It's nice to meet you all. Thank you for all the help today."

"You're most welcome," Mia assured her. She looked thoughtful as she sipped her tea. "If you're looking for some good mountain views, I recommend going up the mountain on Turnback Road. Once your car is fixed up, of course."

"I'll make sure I do that," Bonnie replied. She set her empty mug down on the table. "Do you have a mechanic in the area you would recommend? Once the rain stops, I'll call for a tow."

"There's no need to do that," Dylan said quickly. "We have plenty of people here at the ranch that can fix your car. Besides, this storm isn't going to let up for a while."

"It isn't?" Bonnie felt her heart sink. She had planned on just getting back on the road as soon as possible. She didn't really have a plan on where she was going, but she wanted to keep moving before *they* found her.

Mia shook her head. "The forecast has the rain going until morning, but you should stay here."

"Here?" Bonnie looked around at the cafeteria. It was obviously meant for children and teens, not adults. The colors were far too bright and cheerful.

"All the campers are gone for the night," Mia explained. "We have an extra counselor cabin and plenty of room."

"I really don't want to impose," Bonnie replied. She adjusted the towel on her shoulders. She already felt like they'd done more than needed to help her.

"It's no trouble at all," Dylan assured her. Her eyes went back to him, and she found it hard to look away. He was strong and safe. "There's no reason for you to wait for a tow and spend the night in a hotel."

"And to be honest, the hotel in town isn't all that great," Laura whispered loud enough for the whole room to hear.

"Are you guys sure?" Bonnie looked around the table at the people who barely knew her but were willing to put her up for the night. "You don't know me."

Mia reached across the table and touched her hand. "I know people." Their eyes met, and Bonnie saw only kindness in her eyes. "Stay the night."

"Thank you," Bonnie whispered. She thought about saying no, but the idea of a real bed and a hot shower was too much to pass up. Thunder rumbled outside again, sealing her decision. "I'll stay. Thank you."

"Of course. It's kind of our mission to help people here," Mia explained with a chuckle. "You need some help, so we're here to do that."

"Is there anything I can do to repay you? I'm afraid I don't have a lot of cash right now, but I'd be happy to clean dishes in the kitchen or clean cabins or something," Bonnie offered. "I don't really have a job right now, so I'm happy to help out if you can use me."

Mia started to laugh.

"Fate. It's fate," Laura said, shaking her head and chuckling. "Tell the universe you need something, and there it is."

"Our dishwasher just broke, and we're short-staffed in the kitchen this week," Mia explained. "We need someone to help in the kitchen. I'm afraid it would only be for room and board, but if you want a job, it's yours."

"I want it," Bonnie replied, nearly stumbling over the words in her haste to claim the position. Her funds were running low, and this place would be perfect to hide out in. She took a breath and smiled. "I would really like the job," she repeated, this time with more grace.

"You're sure?" Mia asked, keeping her smile in check. "There's no money."

"It would be amazing," Bonnie told her. "Honestly, room and board is perfect."

It meant less money spent, and it was less likely to be tracked. She couldn't have asked for a better option. Not to mention that it meant she'd probably see more of Dylan. She told herself that wasn't part of her excitement at all.

"Okay." Mia smiled big and wide. "Tomorrow morning, just come back here at seven. Chef will show you the ropes."

"Thank you." Bonnie felt giddy with relief and excitement. Not only did she have a place to stay for the night, but she also had a job for the week. She couldn't have asked for a better place for her car to break down. "I can't tell you how much I appreciate this."

"I'm here to help people," Mia replied with a big smile. "That's what we do here. It looks like you could use the help, so you came to the right place."

Bonnie glanced around the cafeteria as thunder rumbled outside.

You have no idea how right you are, she thought to herself. She needed all the help she could get.

Chapter 4

THE RAIN WAS slow and gentle as he opened the passenger door of the ranch truck for Bonnie. She smiled gratefully as he held the umbrella up over her head as she stepped out into the dark and walked over to her trunk to get her things for the night. Thunder groaned in the distant, but it wasn't threatening.

He held the umbrella up over the two of them as she dug around in the trunk for her suitcase. The rain misted around them as he created their own little dry world for just the two of them. It had almost a magical quality to it.

"Here, let me hold that," he said, taking a red duffle-bag from her and putting it over his shoulder. It was lighter than he thought it would be. She traveled light.

"Thanks." Her cheeks flushed slightly, and she quickly looked back to the car. "I just need to find my toiletry kit."

She turned and dug through the luggage in her trunk.

There were several bags and suitcases, all neatly stacked and arranged in the back. He tried not to stare as she bent over, giving him the perfect view of her ass. He averted his eyes and instead checked out the car.

It was an old brown station wagon that had certainly seen better days. The cloth interior was faded and smelled of air freshener. He wondered just how many miles the thing had on it because it certainly looked ancient.

It was not a good car to be driving through the mountains. He was surprised she'd managed to drive it off the lot, let alone up the highway, given what he could see. The temp tags on her bumper told him she'd just purchased it recently, and he suspected that she had no idea she'd gotten a lemon.

She was trying to escape her old life and had bought a used car to make her escape. Whoever had sold her this car must have known she was desperate and realized they could get this piece of junk off their lot.

The idea that someone had taken advantage of her made his jaw tighten. His hand curled around the strap of the duffel bag. He looked out into the darkness and away from the car to calm himself down. There wasn't anything he could do about it now. He was just going to have to make sure he fixed it up so she wouldn't get stuck on the side of a mountain ever again. Even if it meant building her a new engine.

"Found it," she said, pulling out a small black toiletry bag and holding it up triumphantly. "It was hiding under the blanket."

"If you needed a toothbrush, I know Mia keeps a bunch on hand. Our campers are always loosing or forgetting theirs," he said.

"I already feel like I'm taking advantage," she replied,

motioning for her bag. He handed it to her, and she slid the toiletry kit inside. "Thank you for holding that. And the umbrella. You didn't have to come out here in the rain, and I appreciate it."

"I wasn't about to let you walk around out here in the dark," he told her, the protective urge rising in his chest again. "There are bears and mountain lions out here."

"They like to go out in the rain?" she teased, looking out at the steady downpour.

"Sure," he said with a shrug. "That's where the expression 'it's raining like cats and bears' comes from."

She laughed. The sound was sweet as a bell and made his whole body feel lighter. That laugh alone made coming out in the rain worth it.

She closed the trunk behind her, and he held the umbrella up over the two of them as they walked back to the truck. She stayed close to him, trying to keep dry, and he could feel her body heat reaching for him. He was careful not to touch her, despite the intense desire to wrap his arm around her shoulder and keep her warm.

She was running from an abusive ex, after all.

He'd left the truck running so the heat would be on when they got back inside, so the cab was toasty and comfortable as they climbed in. She smiled at him as he put the truck into drive and headed back down the road.

"Is there a way onto the ranch from this road?" she asked. "I was actually curious why we went the long way."

"There's a gate about a mile up from your car that lets onto the property," Dylan explained. "It's a pain to use, so we keep it permanently locked. There's no reason for cars to be coming up the back way and we'd like to keep it to only one entrance for the kids."

"That makes sense," she agreed. "I guess I'm glad I broke down where I did, or I would never have found you."

He glanced over to see her bite her lip.

"I mean, you guys. The ranch," she amended. "Not you personally. That would be way too forward."

He smiled to himself. She liked him. "If you give me your keys, I'll have your car towed up to the ranch garage tomorrow morning. I can take a look at it and see what needs to be fixed."

"That would be great. Thank you." She reached into her pocket and carefully pulled out a set of keys and removed a giant silver key. The car was so old it didn't have the electronic fobs. She only hesitated a split second before setting it on the center console.

She cleared her throat.

"So, are you from around here?" she asked, her tone light.

"Not really." He turned off the dirt road and onto the highway that would lead them back to the ranch road. "I grew up in Kansas but worked in California for the past few years. I recently quit my job and was looking for something better to do than just waste money. I know Mia and Carter, and they said they could use some help around the ranch, so I came here."

"Mia must collect stray people," she commented.

Dylan chuckled. "You could say that. She has a knack for finding people that need her though. She's certainly good at it."

"Do you like it here?" she asked, turning to look at him in her seat. He could feel her dark eyes examining him as he drove.

"I do," he told her. "At first, I wasn't sure it was what I

needed, but the longer I've stayed, the more I've found that this place is magic."

Bonnie smiled. "That bodes well for me," she replied. Her head cocked to the side, and a damp tendril of hair fell onto her cheek. "What kind of work did you do before coming here?"

"Computers," he replied, keeping the answer short. He looked over at her. "What kind of work did you do?"

"I'm a special needs kindergarten teacher. I work primarily with autism and sensory issues," she replied. Her eyes went soft, and she smiled as she said the words. It was obvious she loved her job. Sadness crept into her face, and the softness left her eyes. "I mean, I was."

"Why'd you leave it?" he asked. She wrapped her arms around herself as she turned to look out her window. He wanted to smack himself upside the head. "Sorry. You had to leave because of your ex. Sorry. Stupid question."

"It's okay. But, yeah." She kept her face turned toward the passenger window. "I had to quit my job. Luckily, it's summer, so they'll be able to fill the position before school starts."

"I'm sorry," he told her. He wanted to reach across the center console and squeeze her hand, but he wasn't sure how she'd react. So he kept his hands on the wheel.

"It is what it is," she said with a shrug. "I'm sure I'll find something like it again."

He hated the way her voice fell and her smile faded. He could see how much her work meant to her and how much it hurt her to leave it. She was passionate about something. He was searching for that feeling himself, so the fact that she couldn't follow her passion made him want to murder her ex for doing this to her.

He pulled the truck up to the counselor cabin and

turned off the engine before hurrying over to her door with the umbrella again. He offered her his hand to get out.

"Thank you," she said softly as she got out of the big truck. She took his hand, sending pleasant electrical surges up his arms with her touch. She didn't hold on once she was on the ground, though.

"Here's the cabin," he said, leaning the umbrella on the porch and opening up the heavy wooden door. "It's a little sparse, but it's comfortable. Your room's over here."

He opened the first door on the right and switched on the light. It was a simple room with just a twin bed, a nightstand, and a dresser with a mirror. An Ansel Adams black and white photograph hung on the wall across from the window.

"It's perfect," she whispered as she stepped into the room. "Absolutely perfect."

He set her duffle-bag on the floor by the bed as she went to the window. It was too dark to see anything except a flash of lighting silhouetting the pine trees outside. She turned and grinned at him.

"The bathroom is the third door on the left," he explained. "You're the only person in this cabin this week, so you've got the place to yourself."

"A hot shower sounds amazing," she told him. He noticed her shoulders relaxing and the anxiety leaving the corners of her eyes.

"There's towels in the bathroom," he explained. "Just put them in the bins when you're done."

"Thank you, Dylan."

The way she said his name sent a thrill up his spine. He tried not to let his voice crack with the surprise of how nice it was to hear her say it.

"Here's my phone number in case you need anything."

He reached into his back pocket and pulled out a business card. It was one of the last habits of his old job that he couldn't quite seem to kick. He loved having business cards for people to contact him. "Just in case."

She took the card and looked it over. It was just his name on white stationery with his private phone number underneath, but she smiled like it was something special he'd given her.

"Thanks," she said, putting it carefully on her nightstand.

He nodded and headed back out to the truck. The rain was still falling, but he didn't care. He left the umbrella on the porch just in case she needed it again. He turned on the engine and smiled to himself as he turned to head back to his own cabin.

She was safe here.

Chapter 5

onnie

SHE TOSSED AND TURNED, throwing blankets off the small bed. Her eyes fluttered behind closed lids as her brain brought images into being. Memories came back as dreams, surreal and yet so lifelike she could no longer tell if she was dreaming or awake. It was happening again.

THE WHOLE STREET was watching the firefighters combat the fire. She'd seen the smoke all the way from the coffee shop. She'd followed the sounds of sirens and the smell of char to find her home wreathed in flames. It was definitely the townhouse she and her younger brother shared.

And it was gone.

She pushed her way past her neighbors up to the police line and watched as her world burned. It was the physical manifestation of what the last few days felt like. Everything in their home was gone. Everything they had was lost. She wasn't sure what she was going to do next.

The acrid smell of burnt plastic filled her nose. She was just glad her brother Brett wasn't there to see this. He was safe and hopefully didn't know all his things were on fire. She was glad she wasn't going to have to be the one to tell him his collection of video games was gone. He was going to flip out.

The small hairs on the back of her neck stood up. It wasn't just the fire that had her edgy. Someone was watching her. She turned slowly. It felt like she was moving through honey. *He* was watching her. She had seen him before. He had dark hair speckled with gray, a perfectly trimmed goatee, and aviator sunglasses. There was a distinctive scar across his right cheek that stood out pale against his tan skin.

The world went cold. Her breathing came fast and uneven. She felt like a rabbit cornered by a wolf. She wasn't safe here.

He made sure she knew he saw her. He made sure she saw him point to the fire and then at himself. Then he pointed at her. A slow, cruel smile moved across his face.

And suddenly, he was gone. He was smoke in the wind.

But the hateful smile remained in her mind.

BONNIE AWOKE PANTING WITH FEAR. In the dark, she couldn't remember where she was. Nothing was familiar. She wasn't in her room at home. She reached for her phone and knocked it to the floor. It was so dark she couldn't see her hand in front of her face as she scrambled down to find it.

She dropped to the floor, her knees cold against the short carpet as her fingers searched and finally found the plastic case.

Her phone screen glowed blue in the night, illuminating the plain bed and nightstand. Memory flooded back to her as she sagged against the bed. She was still safe. She was at the ranch. The fire was just a nightmare. The man, he was real, but he wasn't here.

Bonnie sucked in a jagged breath and forced herself to take another. Her heart was pounding in her chest, and she could still see that smile promising death.

It took a good minute of focusing only on breathing to calm down. She concentrated on the feel of the firm carpet beneath her fingers and the sound of crickets outside her window. Finally, her heart rate slowed from outrunning death to just an intense cardio workout.

She wasn't there any more, in front of that burning house. Now, she was here, in this idyllic mountain town. *They* didn't know where she'd gone, and she was determined to keep it that way. She was going to keep her brother safe.

The room was now a pale gray, and she could make out the details on the dresser. She stood up and stretched, feeling her tight muscles complain and then relax. She didn't want to go back to sleep. She wanted to get to work and have something to keep her mind off things, but work didn't start for another two hours.

Instead, she went and put on her running shoes and workout clothes. If she couldn't work, she could go for a run. She could focus on music and run the crazy off. She was already covered in sweat, so she was going to need a shower before work anyway.

She glanced at her reflection in the mirror over her

dresser and didn't recognize the woman standing there. The hair was shorter and darker. She'd made sure to change up her appearance to make it harder to spot her in a crowd.

"Might as well burn the calories," she told herself as she bent over and laced up her shoes. She stepped out into the crisp morning air and took a deep breath. It smelled of clean pine and morning dew. The fire was becoming a memory again. She put her music on speaker and started to run along the path to the barn.

With every step, the fire faded from her mind, and she let the mountains give her peace.

Chapter 6

onnie

SUNLIGHT FLICKERED and danced through the pine boughs, and birds sang squeaky melodies as Bonnie walked along the gravel path to the cafeteria building. The long thin grass was still wet from the night's rain, and everything smelled of wet pine and fresh dirt. She took a deep breath in and immediately felt like she was where she was supposed to be.

The path to the cafeteria flat and easy to walk, but with a view of the Rocky Mountains that took her breath away. The mountains were so much bigger and grander than she had imagined. It was so different from New Jersey that it felt like she'd stepped through a magic mirror and into a world of myth. A friendly little squirrel chattered at her from the top of a bright green pine tree as she walked past. She was fairly certain if she burst into song, the squirrel would sing the melody with her just like in a princess movie.

She turned a corner to find the large building that housed the cafeteria and kitchen. The big wooden structure stood at the heart of the camp with all the gravel paths leading toward the center where food and fun could be found. From here, she could see a barn, a garage, and several smaller structures she assumed were the bunks for campers.

None of the children of the camp were up and about yet, but Dylan was. She could see him in the open garage.

He was under the hood of her ancient station wagon, his hands deep in the engine. The car, and the handsome man working on it were in a large open garage filled with all sorts of shiny tools. She wondered just how many cars broke down around here to justify a garage like that. It was huge and definitely nicer than the mechanic she took her car to at home.

The garage wasn't on her path to the cafeteria building, and she couldn't see a way to walk over there without making it very clear that she was looking for him. She liked him, but she didn't want to appear desperate. Besides, she didn't want to be late for her first day on the job. Still, she couldn't help but glance over as she walked.

Dylan had on ripped jeans that hugged the curves of his body and looked like they were made just for him. His light blue t-shirt already dirty with grease and a long cloth hung from his pocket. The angle of his body gave her the perfect view of his very muscular ass as he leaned over to work on her engine.

Heat fluttered in her low belly. She wasn't usually a car girl but seeing a handsome man working on her car was something to be enjoyed. She did her best not to stare but still managed to nearly trip at least three times as she walked because she wasn't watching her feet.

All too soon, she found herself on the front porch of the cafeteria. The wood was still damp from the rain as she climbed the three steps up to the two big heavy doors and stepped inside.

The eating area was better lit now that it was full of sunshine, but it still held the warmth and friendship from the night before. All the tables were set out with extra napkins, and she knew the children would be ready to eat soon.

"Hello?" she called out, unsure if she should head to the kitchen to find a guide. For a second, she thought about going and asking Dylan, if only for the chance to speak to him again.

"Oh, you're early!" A voice echoed through the empty space. Bonnie searched until a face popped out from behind one of the swinging kitchen doors. She had long dark hair pulled up into a ponytail and a friendly smile.

"Hi." Bonnie waved and walked over to the door. The young woman came out and shook her hand.

"Hi, I'm Elena," the woman told her. "I'm one of the volunteers here. You must be Bonnie. Mia asked me to show you around. Come on into the kitchen."

Elena held open the swinging kitchen door for Bonnie to enter. The kitchen was already bustling with life. Two chefs were hard at work chopping and stirring and bustling around the brightly lit kitchen. Everything was stainless steel and sunshine.

"You'll be working back here in the kitchen," Elena explained, leading toward the back of the large space. "The dishwasher broke, and since it's an industrial one, they won't have the part in until tomorrow. We'll need you to hand wash these."

She turned and motioned to a large stainless steel sink.

There were only a couple of dishes and pots, but Bonnie had a feeling that it was going to get full quickly once the campers started eating.

"I can do that," Bonnie said cheerfully. If washing dishes got her a place to sleep and food to eat, she was happy to do it. It was better than any alternative she had right now.

"When you're not washing, if you want to help Chef out, she'll love you forever," Elena replied. "Come on over and meet her."

Elena brought Bonnie over to a large woman in what Bonnie guessed was her late sixties. She stirred the biggest pot of oatmeal Bonnie had ever seen with ease. The woman had her silver hair piled up in a giant braid wrapping around her head. As the woman turned to greet them, she gave Bonnie a giant, friendly grin.

"Chef, this is Bonnie," Elena announced.

The woman stopped stirring and beamed another smile. "It's so nice to meet you, Bonnie. Just call me Chef, that's what I have everyone call me," she told her. "We've got oatmeal and pancakes for the kids this morning, soup and sandwiches for lunch, and spaghetti for dinner."

Bonnie did the mental math of dishes in her head. She was going to be doing a lot of washing.

"Now, we do some special orders," Chef continued. "Coming here is a big transition for most of these kids, so we try to make things as gentle as possible, especially the first few days. Kids can request grilled cheese sandwiches or hot-dogs, which are right here."

Chef pulled open a stainless steel fridge handle to show row upon row of cheese blocks and hot-dogs. In neat containers on a separate shelf were different kinds of fruit and veggies. Each was neatly labeled and ready for hungry children.

"They're also allowed to have as many fruits and veggies as they'd like," Chef told her. "Most kids like the meals here, but like I said, this camp is a big change for a lot of them, and we'd rather they eat something than force them to try something new and cause a meltdown."

Bonnie nodded. "I've worked with special needs kids. One of the first things to go for many of them when they get stressed is the ability to try new foods," Bonnie replied. "For kids with sensory issues, it's really hard to try new things, and even familiar foods can be hard when changing environments and schedules."

Chef beamed another megawatt grin at her. "You sound just like Mia," she said with a laugh. She picked up her oatmeal spoon and began stirring again. "If you have any questions, just let me or my staff know."

"Thank you, Chef," Bonnie replied.

"If you'll come with me, I have some paperwork for you to fill out," Elena said, tapping her on the shoulder. "You should be able to fill it out before breakfast starts, and the dishes roll in."

Bonnie nodded and followed Elena off to a back office. It was neat and clean with pictures of kids lining the walls. Bonnie assumed it was Chef's office. Laid out on the desk was a small stack of papers and a pen all ready for her to fill out and sign.

"Oh, I'm supposed to tell you that you're not to interact with the kids," Elena said as Bonnie sat down and began to read over the forms. She shrugged apologetically. "It's a legal thing."

Bonnie waved her hand through the air. "I totally get it. You need a background check to work with kids."

Elena looked surprised. "Yeah. How'd you know that?"

"I work with kids. I was a special needs teacher before I

came here," Bonnie replied with a smile before focusing back on the papers in front of her. She could feel Elena watching her and looked up to see a thoughtful look cross the other woman's face.

"Interesting," Elena murmured. "Anyway, go ahead and fill these out and I'll get them filed, scanned, and submitted. I'll be back in just a few minutes."

"Okay," Bonnie replied with a smile. She worked on filling out her name and birth dates on the form for a few minutes. When she got to her last job, she paused. She was almost afraid to put information down in case it would lead her past back to her. She paused, her pen hovering over the blank spaces.

She looked up and out the window in the small office. From here, she could see her car in the garage as well as the man working on it. He had a dark smear of grease across his cheek as he walked around to try and start the engine.

It was sexy as hell.

"I wonder if he's single," she murmured to herself. Bonnie shook her head. Even if he was, it didn't matter. She couldn't stay here for long. It wasn't safe for her to stay in one spot for too long. They were looking for her. She was the way to get to her brother. She was his weakness. They would hurt her in order to get to him to not testify.

She shivered and looked at the blank spaces. She left some of them blank that weren't critical to her history. It would be complete enough, she reasoned. For references, she just put in her old boss. He knew her story and would keep her background safe.

She couldn't get involved here. As much as she enjoyed watching the muscular man with grease on his cheek work on her car, it wasn't safe to get attached. She had to keep herself separate from these people, no matter how kind they were.

She sighed and forced her eyes back to her paper. This was how her life was now.

Chapter 7

onnie

"MIA?" Bonnie called out, jogging across the pale green grass. It wasn't a lawn to Bonnie's eyes, but it was a patch of grass, although it had a lot of weeds too. It was bare in some spots and lush in others with long stems peeking out wherever the mower had missed them. It looked wild and rustic.

Bonnie's feet hurt from standing in the kitchen all day. The sun was just coming to touch the mountains and disappear for the evening. It was still early, but she was ready to take a shower and head straight to bed. Washing dishes was hard work.

"Hi, Bonnie," Mia greeted her, turning from the path. She had her daughter tucked into a baby carrier attached to her chest. The tiny baby girl was snuggled up against her mother's chest fast asleep. "Dylan says that your car's fixed for now. It was something to do with the engine, but I don't remember what he said it was. It's just a temporary fix though. He says he needs to get a new part to make it actually work right."

"How much do I owe him?" Bonnie asked. She had no idea what it would cost to fix something like that. Given the way her brother refused to let anyone but his friend work on his cars, she had a feeling it was rather expensive.

"No charge," Mia replied, waving her hand through the air with a smile. She leaned forward. "I think he rather enjoyed it."

Bonnie wasn't sure what to say to that. A free mechanic? She wasn't about to look a gift horse in the mouth, but she was certainly surprised. Hopefully, it wasn't too expensive a repair. She didn't want to take advantage of their kindness.

"So, how'd your first day go?" Mia asked, adjusting the baby on her chest. She smiled as she smoothed the fabric across the baby's back. The baby just dozed on.

"I was actually hoping to talk to you about something," Bonnie replied. She tucked a strand of hair behind her ear. "They said you were the person to ask."

"Um, sure?" Mia replied with a nervous chuckle. "I try not to manage Chef, though. If you have an issue, you need to bring it up with her."

"Oh no, Chef is fantastic," Bonnie quickly replied. "She's the one who told me to bring my idea to you."

"Oh, okay." Mia relaxed. "What do you have in mind?"

Bonnie took a deep breath. "I noticed we have a lot of picky eaters. I think I made a million grilled cheeses tonight, even though there was spaghetti. A lot of the kids just didn't seem sure about it."

"It happens a lot the first couple of days of camp," Mia assured her. "We try to pick something most kids like, but we can't please everyone."

"Well, we have a ton of spaghetti noodles left over, and I

was wondering if we could use it to make a spaghetti pool."
Bonnie held her breath. She wasn't sure if Mia was going to
go for her idea. She had the feeling the Mia was open to new
things, but Bonnie also didn't want to overstep her bounds.
She had a good thing here, and she didn't want to mess
anything up.

"A what?" Mia asked, looking totally confused.

"A spaghetti pool. We used to do it for our sensory kids
that struggled with food," Bonnie explained. "We'd fill a
kiddie-pool with noodles and just let the kids play with it.
They don't have to eat it unless they want to. It's just for
playing with. It really helped take the fear out of food. They
could squish it and play with it. Since we have so much left
over, I thought we could do it here."

Mia looked impressed. "A spaghetti pool... I like it," she
said softly. She started to nod and then looked carefully at
Bonnie. "Elena said you have a childcare background?"

"A degree in special education," Bonnie told her.

"I love it. I'll tell Elena to set it up in the morning." Mia
smiled. "Thanks."

Mia seemed pleased with the idea, so Bonnie continued.
"I have some other ideas if you want them. I primarily
worked with autism and sensory processing disorder, so I
have a lot of experience with coming up with sensory-
friendly play."

"How many years experience?" Mia asked.

"Just over five years," Bonnie answered. "Plus college
experience."

Mia nodded, looking thoughtful. "You filled out the
background check sheet, right?" she asked. "Elena got you in
our system?"

"I filled out as much of it as I could," Bonnie explained.
"Given my situation."

"Right." Mia tipped her head and evaluated her for a moment before smiling. "We might have something for you that isn't in the kitchen. If you're interested."

A flutter of excitement filled Bonnie's chest. Helping kids was what she lived for. She had been so excited to ask Mia about the spaghetti pool, and she had so many other ideas after seeing what the kids were eating. There was so much she could help with.

"I'd love to!" Bonnie grinned, then pulled it back. She had to remember why she was here. "But, I did tell you that I'm kind of on the run. I can't guarantee how long I'll be able to stay here."

Mia frowned. "You know we can help you with that, right? We have a lot of resources around here."

"Thank you, but it's complicated." If that wasn't the understatement of the year, Bonnie wasn't sure what was.

"It always is," Mia agreed. Mia checked her baby to make sure she was still sleeping and then looked over at Bonnie. It felt like she could peer straight into Bonnie's soul and see exactly what she had hidden there. "I'm going to take a chance on you, Bonnie. I have a pretty good track record with people, and I have a good feeling about you."

"Are you sure?" Bonnie asked. She fiddled with her hands in front of her. "I mean, I would love to work with these kids, but I just don't want to put you in a difficult position if I have to leave suddenly."

Mia chuckled. "One thing I've learned since starting this is that there's always some sort of difficult position with everyone. Employees are hard work."

"Thank you for believing in me, Mia," Bonnie said softly.

Mia reached out and put her hand on Bonnie's shoulder and smiled. It was the first time since leaving the police station she'd let someone get close enough to touch her. It was nice to have the connection. She'd missed interacting with people, and she was surprised by just how much the simple touch made her chest ache for friendship and belonging.

"I'll let you know when your background check clears." Mia smiled and then turned to continue her walk. "Keep on working hard. I'll see you tomorrow."

Bonnie stared after her. Her heart felt heavy and light at the same time, and she wasn't quite sure what to do about it.

Chapter 8

*onnie*

"You go take a break for a bit," Chef told Bonnie, patting her on the shoulder. "You got all the dishes done. Dinner will be soon enough, and it's going to be a doozy."

Bonnie's arms were tired. Her feet were tired. She'd washed dishes all morning, all afternoon, and was preparing herself to wash dinner dishes again this evening. It was hard, but it was worth the room and board.

"That sounds great. Thanks," Bonnie replied, putting her drying towel up on a rack. "What's for dinner?"

"Tacos," Chef informed her. "My secret recipe for the salsa."

"I'm already looking forward to it," Bonnie said. "I mean, the meal. Not the dishes."

Chef laughed. "Go take a break. You've earned it."

Bonnie thanked her and took off her apron. She stepped out into the warm summer mountains sunshine. The scent of pine was almost overwhelming, but it was dry and pleasant. There was no humidity up here, even after all the rain.

She walked past the garage, sad to see that Dylan wasn't in it working. She'd enjoyed peeking out the kitchen window to see him up to his elbows in grease as he worked on her car. He had some of the older camp kids helping him out during the day as they fixed up cars and farm vehicles.

She liked a man that could work with his hands. If he saw her walking past, he would always smile and wave. Yesterday, he'd even invited her to come to the garage if she wanted.

Bonnie's phone chirped in her pocket. She looked down to see that it was a calendar reminder to check her email. She grinned and hurried back to her cabin. It was mail day.

She made sure the door was securely locked behind her. It didn't really matter, but it made her feel safer nonetheless. She found the laptop she'd bought in Kentucky on her way here and pulled it out of a bag. It was time to check in on her brother.

She logged into the throwaway email account she'd made for him to contact her. He had one of his own. Waiting in her inbox was an email from Brett. She grinned and opened it up.

Dear Sis,

Things here are good. It's kind of boring right now, so my "friends" are teaching me all about their jobs. I think they are just sick of me beating them at poker every night, but I kind of like it. They say after this is done, I might be able to get a job. I'm seriously thinking about it.

> *Anyway, that's it here. I hope you are safe.*
> *Love you.*

HIS "FRIENDS" were the police officers keeping him safe. She let out a sigh of relief. He was safe.

She opened up a new message.

> *Hey Bro,*
> *Be nice to your new "friends."*
> *Things here are good. I'm safe and far away. It's really beautiful. I'll take you here someday.*
> *I haven't had anything bad happen, so you don't have to worry about me. Things actually seem to be looking up for a change. I'll let you know if anything changes. Until then, stay safe.*
> *Love you.*

THERE WAS SO MUCH MORE that she wanted to write. She wanted to tell him about Dylan and her car. She wanted to let him know that the house and the fire were taken care of. She wanted to tell him that she'd gotten a job and that she was actually verging on being happy, despite everything.

But she didn't dare.

If *they* managed to get their hands on these emails, they could use that information. Neither one of them wanted to risk any extra information getting out, so they made sure to cover their tracks and give as little detail as possible.

So, she didn't tell her brother what was going on in her

life. She hated not being able to talk to him. Even though they were night and day opposites, Brett had her back. He looked out for her, and she looked out for him. They were family.

It was why she was on the run. If *they* captured her, Brett would do anything to save her. He would hold his testimony to keep her safe. She knew that if their situations were reversed, she would do the same. It was what siblings did for one another.

So, since the police couldn't protect her, she was on the run. She was going to keep her brother safe by not being found. She knew she could do it, even though it was hard.

She looked out the small window at the dark green pines and the bright blue sky. She was safe here. They would never find her here. For the first time since the fire, she felt like making it to the trial was possible.

Chapter 9

onnie

BONNIE FELL EFFORTLESSLY into the rhythm of the camp. By day four of working in the kitchen, she was joking with Chef and already knew all the names of the horses in the barn. She worked her tail off washing dishes and making request meals for the camp kids. Anything Chef asked her to do she did as quickly and efficiently as possible.

She felt safe here. There wasn't a whisper of her former life. She secretly started to wish that the part for the dish-washing machine would keep getting delayed. She didn't want to leave this place.

Bonnie picked up another bowl and quickly scrubbed, rinsed, and placed it on the drying rack. Only fifty more bowls to go for lunch, she thought.

She paused and saw Dylan walk past the window with a gaggle of children at his heels. He never seemed to be far from her during the day. She wanted to imagine that it was on purpose, but it was far more likely that he just liked being in the garage or out with the camp kids.

The kitchen doors opened, and Mia strode in right as the lunch rush finished. Today her daughter was with her husband, and she was running around the camp getting things done.

"I have good news and bad news," Mia announced. Everyone turned to look at her. The kitchen became quiet except for the sounds of the food sizzling on the grill and the water filling the sink.

"Well, start with the bad news," Chef replied, crossing her arms across her chest. She held her heavy wooden spoon like a sword.

"Chef, you're losing your human dishwasher," Mia told the kitchen staff. Her face was stern and businesslike. "She can't be in the kitchen anymore."

The news hit Bonnie harder than she had expected it to. She didn't want to leave this place. She knew this was only temporary, but she certainly wasn't ready to go yet. She wasn't ready to run again.

"What?" Chef hurried over to Bonnie and wrapped an arm around her shoulder. Bonnie leaned in, taking strength from the older woman. "No. I like her. She stays, Mia."

"Chef, the dishwasher part came," Mia replied gently. "Dylan's coming to install it now."

"What about Bonnie?" Chef's arm tightened around Bonnie. Bonnie's throat was thick, and she was glad she didn't have to say anything. She wasn't sure if she would be able to say anything without crying.

Mia walked over to stand in front of Chef. Her face twitched with a smile, betraying the stern, business-like look she currently wore.

"That's the good news," Mia told the two of them. "Her background check came through today."

"What?" Bonnie's heart skipped a beat. Why would she be getting fired if her background check came in? What had Mia found?

"Bonnie, if you'd like, I need someone to work with some of our kids. We have a lot of un-diagnosed behavioral issues. It's hard to get a diagnosis for some of these kids, but they need help just the same." Mia's false sternness disappeared, and she grinned. "So, we need someone here to help come up with programming and activities for these high-need kids."

"You want me?" Bonnie whispered, unsure if she understood correctly. "You're giving me a job?"

"After your idea for the spaghetti bath and talking with your old boss, I think you're perfect for the camp. We need someone with your qualifications," Mia confirmed. "Are you interested in staying?"

Bonnie's lower lip trembled, and she felt her eyes starting to fill with relief. "Yes! I would love the job."

Chef's arm tightened around Bonnie into a full-fledged hug. Bonnie wrapped her arms around Chef and hugged her tightly back.

"Thank you so much, Mia," Bonnie said, releasing Chef and facing Mia. She wiped at her cheeks.

"Your boss had the most glowing and amazing things to say about you, Bonnie. She couldn't speak highly enough about how well you work with kids and make them feel safe," Mia replied. "I'm hoping that you can bring that same magic here. We need someone like you."

Guilt pricked at Bonnie's chest for half a second. She was going to have to leave this place eventually. Even if everything with her brother and the mob disappeared, her home was in New Jersey, not Colorado. She had a life there.

She pushed the guilt down hard. For now, she had a place. She had a place where she could use her skills and talents with kids to make their lives better. She wasn't about to turn down this opportunity.

"Thank you, Mia. I promise to do whatever I can." She could keep that promise, she told herself. It wasn't promising to stay. It was just to do what she could.

Mia stepped closer and hugged her. "And I don't want you to worry. I was incredibly discreet with the background check. Your boss doesn't know what state you're in, and I used a different office for all the paperwork addresses. No one can trace you back here," she said quietly into Bonnie's ear.

Bonnie hugged her tightly. "Thank you." Mia had no idea how much it meant that she'd done her best to keep Bonnie safe. It meant more to Bonnie than she could ever say.

"You're welcome," Mia told her, giving her one more squeeze before letting her go. "You start tomorrow. Once Chef lets you go tonight, feel free to explore the camp. You've been cleared to work with kids, so you can enjoy what the camp has to offer."

Excitement bubbled up through Bonnie's chest, and she felt like she might burst into song. She was going to be able to stay at this beautiful place where she felt safe. It was more than she could have asked.

"Okay. Bonnie, I'll see you tomorrow morning in my office to come up with a plan," Mia said. "Everyone else, have a great evening and I won't see you in my office."

Chef and the other two kitchen workers chuckled as Mia left the kitchen. As she left, Dylan replaced her. He wore his soft denim jeans and T-shirt like a work uniform as he held up the small plastic and metal piece for the dishwasher. He smiled at everyone, but Bonnie felt for a moment that he smiled at her the most.

She shook her head as he went to the dishwasher and began taking it apart. She was just high on the job offer and seeing good things everywhere. She glanced over to get the perfect view of him reaching into the machine, his strong arms flexed and his legs braced against the floor as he worked the new piece into place. It was a great view.

She was going to enjoy her new workplace. Especially if Dylan was nearby.

Chapter 10

onnie

ONCE THE DISH-WASHING machine was fixed and loaded with dishes, there wasn't much left for Bonnie to do in the kitchen. She helped with putting the food from lunch away and sweeping the floors before she left. Chef had her promise to stop in and say hello on a regular basis, but then promptly shooed her out of the kitchen to go explore the camp.

Chef had mentioned multiple times how nice the camp pool was after a hard day's work. Now that her background check had cleared, Bonnie felt like she could go to the pool and not be afraid of interacting with the campers. Up until today, she didn't want to go where she wasn't allowed, but with the job offer, the camp opened up to her.

She put on her favorite one-piece swimsuit, a pair of sweatpants, and a light jacket and began to wander the ranch looking for the famed pool.

She found the barn where Laura was teaching some of the older kids how to groom horses. She waved, but since she wasn't dressed for working with animals, continued on her way. She promised herself that she would convince Laura to give her riding lessons one of these days, though. It was too good an opportunity to pass up.

She found the ropes course, a fire pit, a badminton court, a horseshoe pit, and several other outdoor games, but no swimming pool. It was a great camp for the foster kids to gain life skills and have an amazing week where they were special. The more she walked around the camp, the more she shared in Mia's vision to make this place a sanctuary for kids who didn't have families.

Mia's statement the night they met about this being a place to help people, really sunk in. This was a place for hope. This was a place for dreams and love.

She was about to give up and ask for directions when she finally saw it on the far edge of the property.

It was a beautiful pool. There were two lap lanes on the far edge, but the main pool area looked like something out of a travel magazine. The clear blue water had a beach entrance and a small slide shaped like an octopus. A larger yellow slide dropped into the deep end. There was also a hot tub nestled off to the side that bubbled and beckoned her to come and relax.

Two boys jumped into the deep end with a splash. They looked to be around five to six, and both shrieked with delight as they flew through the air and into the water. Elena laughed as the two of them came to the surface and asked her which splash was bigger.

Elena raised a friendly hand in greeting as Bonnie approached. She was busy watching the two boys, so Bonnie didn't want to bother her. Besides, she was more interested in scoping out the pool for a sensory activity. The gentle slope of the beach entrance was perfect for kids afraid of the water. She wondered if they had some pool noodles as well. Pool noodles would be perfect for what she had in mind.

She set her towel on a chair by the edge of the water and walked over to the pool shed. It was just a small building off to the side of the pool that she figured housed the pool supplies. If there were pool noodles, they would be inside.

She pulled open the heavy wooden door and looked around. The inside was neatly organized with pool cleaning equipment on one side and toys on the other. There were some arm floaties hanging on the wall, a couple of deflated beach balls, and about half a dozen pool noodles.

Bonnie grinned. There was so much she could do with this. Her brain buzzed with sensory activities that would help the camp kids feel comfortable in the water and learn to swim. She loved working with water because most kids ended up loving it.

That's when she heard the sniffle.

It was small, but it made all thoughts of pool noodles and activities vanish. She looked around, closing the door and searching for whoever was crying.

Behind the pool shed, sitting on a smooth gray stone was a little boy. He was small and thin with shaggy blonde hair and big brown eyes. As soon as he saw her, he wrapped his arms around himself and shrunk down. His swim trunks were sun-bleached and worn, but the turtles decorating them were still visible. His dark blue sweatshirt was a size too big.

"Hi," she said, taking a step forward and then crouching down, so she was at his height. He looked up at her and then quickly back down at the ground. He wiped his nose with the back of his hand.

"My name's Bonnie. I'm new here." Bonnie gave him a small wave. "What's your name?"

"Tyson," the boy replied, still looking at the ground. "T-Y-S-O-N."

"It's nice to meet you, Tyson. You must be, what? Eight years old?" She purposefully guessed high. The boy couldn't be more than five or six, but kids always seemed to like that they looked older.

He smiled a little. "I'm five. My birthday is next month, and I'll be six then."

"Well then, happy early birthday, Tyson," Bonnie told him.

The boy risked a quick glance up at her before returning his gaze to study the rocks in front of him. He had the longest eyelashes.

Bonnie wasn't sure exactly what question to ask. Many of the kids at this camp were in the foster system, and all of them had a different story. Instead of simply asking *"What's wrong?"*, she decided to go with a gentler question.

"Are you going swimming, Tyson?" Bonnie asked, keeping a friendly smile. "I was going to get in the water, but I'd love to have someone to play with. Would you like to join me?"

The little boy's brow scrunched as he thought about it. He swallowed hard and kept looking down, never meeting her eyes.

"I don't know how to swim," he said quietly. "The other kids just want to jump in."

"Oh, that's okay," Bonnie replied. "I was just going to go in the shallow end anyway."

Tyson fiddled with the string of his hoodie. He looked over at the pool, his eyes focusing on the pretty blue water and then filling with tears he tried to blink away. He obviously wanted to swim but was afraid of something.

"Would you like me to teach you how to swim?" Bonnie asked. "I used to give lessons, and now I teach kindergarten. I can give you my resume if you want."

Two brown eyes flickered up to look at her for a split second. They were the biggest, most beautiful eyes Bonnie had ever seen on a child. The sadness in them broke her heart, and all she wanted to do was scoop up the boy and hug him until his eyes sparkled with joy rather than tears.

"Are you going to make me go underwater?" Tyson asked. His voice was uncertain. "I don't like the way it feels on my ears."

"If you don't want to, then no," Bonnie promised. "You get to be in control of the lesson the whole time."

The boy thought for a moment. "Okay." He wiped at his nose again.

She stood up and stepped over so the boy could walk beside her on the path back to the pool. Together they headed toward the water. It was then that she noticed that *someone* was now swimming laps at the far end.

A *someone* with a great male body. And dark hair. A *someone* named Dylan.

The idea that he was going to see her in her swimsuit made the color rise in her cheeks. She was glad she'd worn the suit that made her feel pretty. He probably wouldn't even notice, she told herself, so she decided to ignore him.

She slipped out of her sweatpants and jacket as Tyson took his jacket off and left it on the chair next to hers. She offered her hand, and he took it as they walked to the edge of the water. He held on tight, betraying just how nervous he felt about this.

"Okay, are you ready?" she asked, the boy. "We're going

to jump into the water and make the biggest splash we can. Do you think you can make a bigger splash than me?"

A flicker of a smile crossed his face. "I'm gonna win."

"Okay." She took a deep breath and made a big show of jumping into the shallow water. Since it was a graded beach entrance, she only landed in about six inches of water but managed to make a decent splash. She was pleased to find the pool was heated to a comfortable temperature. "Beat that."

Tyson let out a whoop and used every ounce of his small frame to propel himself up and into the shallow water. His splash was messy, but he grinned as he looked at her. He wasn't so afraid. She was going to make sure he kept this new confidence.

"That was awesome!" she told him. "I think you beat me. Are you sure you don't know how to swim? You seem like a natural."

He smiled wide and shook his head.

"Okay. Let's go a little deeper." She took a couple of steps until the water lapped at her mid-thigh.

From the corner of her eye, she saw Dylan stop at the end of his lap and take his goggles off. His eyes were a warm heat on her back, and she tried not to let it fluster her. Just because he was looking didn't mean anything.

"Come to me, Tyson," Bonnie encouraged. She dropped to her knees, so the water hit her upper stomach.

Tyson's smile faded a little with every step into the deeper water, but he made it to her. The water lapped at his chest. He smiled weakly as he came to a stop.

"You're doing great," she told him. "The next step to swimming is to blow bubbles. Like this."

She took in a dramatic breath and put her mouth and

nose in the water and blew out a steady stream of large bubbles.

"See? And my ears didn't go in the water." She showed him her dry ears. "Your turn."

Tyson frowned, but he took a deep breath and put his chin in the water. Immediately, he pulled up and away from the water. "I can't do it."

"Are you sure? I think you can," Bonnie replied. "What if we just made little bubbles first?"

"You can do it because you're a girl," Tyson told her, crossing his arms. "It's harder for boys."

"Oh. So you need a boy to show you how it's done?" she asked.

"Yeah." He looked pleased with himself, thinking that he had found a way to keep from doing something difficult.

"Okay." Bonnie turned to the lap lane where Dylan was watching the two of them work. "Hey, Dylan? Will you come blow some bubbles with us?"

Dylan grinned and ducked his head under the lap lane rope. He quickly crossed the length of the pool to join them in the shallow water. He knelt next to Bonnie. She had to tell herself not to stare at his chest and abs. He definitely worked out, and it showed. She was just glad that most of him was underwater.

"So, we're blowing bubbles?" Dylan asked. "I'm a bubble master."

He took a deep breath and put his mouth in the water and blew an impressive stream of bubbles. Tyson watched him, but his worried expression didn't change.

"See? Boys can totally do it," Bonnie told him. She watched him for a moment and remembered that Tyson didn't like water on his ears. "Are you scared of the water getting on you?"

"What if it gets in my eyes and I can't see?" Tyson asked. "This water hurts my eyes."

"I bet Dylan will let you borrow his goggles," Bonnie told him.

"Of course," Dylan said. He pulled the goggles off is head and helped Tyson put them on. "Plus, these are magic goggles."

"Magic goggles?" Tyson asked. He looked like an adorable water creature with big eyes wearing Dylan's goggles.

"Yup." Dylan nodded solemnly. "They let you hold your breath for three seconds longer underwater. I got them from a mermaid."

Tyson felt the goggles with his fingertips and grinned. "Okay."

He took a deep breath, hesitated and then touched the goggles before putting his face in the water and blowing. Bubbles came fast and short, but he managed to get bubbles under the water before quickly standing again.

"Fantastic!" Dylan and Bonnie both praised him. "Do it again!"

Tyson grinned, looking back and forth between the two of them. "Okay!" His confidence was multiplying, and Bonnie was pleased.

This time, Tyson didn't hesitate. He blew a great stream of bubbles into the water, his fear lessening with every second. He lifted his head, pride at his bubbles radiating of his small frame.

"You're doing great," Bonnie praised. "I don't think I've ever seen better bubbles."

"Tyson?" Elena called from the edge of the pool. The two boys who were jumping in earlier were wrapped in towels next to her. "Are you ready to come get some dinner?"

Tyson looked over at Bonnie and then to Dylan. "Um... no."

"We got him," Dylan said, putting his arm around Tyson. "We'll make sure he gets to the cafeteria for dinner."

Something about the way Dylan said, *"we"* made Bonnie's insides flutter. She liked being a *"we"* with him.

"Okay. We'll see you guys there. Thanks, Dylan. Bye Bonnie." Elena waved and then began to guide the two boys with her toward the kid's cabins.

"How'd they get Tyson in the water?" one of the boys asked Elena as they walked. "He's scared of it."

"I don't know," Elena replied. "But isn't it great?"

"Yeah," the other boy replied with a grin. "We need another person to play Marco Polo with. It's no fun with just two."

Their voices faded as the three of them got further and further away from the pool. Bonnie turned back to focus on Tyson. He looked so happy with his goggles taking up most of his small face.

"So, bubbles are how we talk to the fish of the pool," Bonnie explained. "Next, we have to work on catching them!"

Tyson giggled. "But there's no fish in the pool."

"Are you sure?" Dylan asked, looking around and pointing to invisible fish. "You don't see them? I see a rainbow fish and a dinosaur fish. I'm going to catch a... hippopotamus fish!"

Tyson laughed, getting into the game. "Okay. How do we catch a hippo-ta... a hippotatumus... hippopotamus fish?"

"Like this." Bonnie put one arm out in front of her and dove it into the water, repeating the motion on the opposite side. It was basically the doggy-paddle. "You try."

Both Dylan and Tyson mimicked her motions, with Dylan splashing as much as possible.

"I'm going to catch a Tyson fish!" Bonnie called out, moving to tickle Tyson. The boy giggled and used the new swimming motion to move away from her.

"I'm going to catch a Dylan fish!" Tyson yelled. He moved his arms through the water and Dylan let him catch him. He ducked under the water and then came up, his dark hair wet. With an easy motion, he pushed his hair out of his eyes and Bonnie had a hard time not looking at the way his biceps flexed when he did it.

"Bonnie fish!" Tyson and Dylan yelled at the same time. She tried to get away, but they both caught her and dunked her. She came up laughing.

They played this game for a while. Dylan and Bonnie took turns going underwater if Tyson caught them, but they never dunked him. They had him blow bubbles and practice putting his face in the water, but they didn't push him past what he was comfortable with.

Bonnie loved it when Dylan caught her. His hands on her shoulders as he pushed her into the water were strong and gentle. He didn't force her, but rather guided her down. She was enjoying having him touch her. It was a long time since anyone had touched her, even as a friend and it felt nice to be close to someone.

"Okay, who's hungry?" Dylan asked, coming up after being caught. "It's time for dinner, and I'm hungry. Tyson fish and Bonnie fish are fun, but I need food!"

Tyson retreated slightly. He wasn't about to give up on this game without a fight. "I'm not ready to eat yet. I'm having fun."

Bonnie glanced at her watch. It was almost past when

Chef made food. They needed to get Tyson to the cafeteria soon if he was going to eat tonight.

"How about another lesson tomorrow?" she offered.

"Promise?" Tyson asked. He pushed the goggles from his eyes and onto the top of his head. Red rings circled his eyes like a raccoon's markings, somehow making him even cuter.

"Promise," she replied. "Same place, same time."

"You too, Dylan?" Tyson asked, turning to the man next to him.

Dylan looked up at Bonnie and grinned. "If you want me to, I'm here."

"I want you to come too," Tyson told him.

Bonnie's heart skipped a beat. She wanted Dylan to come too.

"Then I'm here," Dylan told him.

"Okay." Tyson nodded, handed Dylan his goggles and got out of the pool without further pushing. He wrapped himself up in his towel and looked at the two of them like they were crazy for still being in the water.

"Are you two coming or what?" Tyson asked, slipping on his sandals and starting to walk toward the cafeteria. "It's dinnertime."

Dylan looked over at Bonnie and laughed. "I guess he's hungry."

Bonnie chuckled as they both hurried out of the swimming pool to catch up with Tyson.

Chapter 11

 *ylan*

Tyson took the seat next to Elena and happily dug into his grilled cheese sandwich. The boy ate like he was starving, and given the way he'd been swimming, Dylan wasn't surprised. The boy gave him a grin and a wave before concentrating on his meal.

"You did great with him," Bonnie said as the two of them headed toward the kitchen to get their own dinner. Her sweatpants had the distinct wet outline of her swimsuit on her ass and chest. He was having a hard time not staring at those beautiful wet spots.

She had made sure Tyson had changed into dry pajamas before coming to dinner, but neither Dylan nor Bonnie had changed out of their wet swimsuits yet. They wanted to get Tyson to dinner first. Dylan was trying not to enjoy the fact that it made Bonnie's assets very apparent in spite of her concealing sweats.

"Thanks," he replied, navigating around a table full of kids. "You're the one who did most of the work. I'm impressed."

She chuckled. "A lot of these kids have come from tough situations, but this kid seems easy to work with."

"That's not exactly true," he told her, shaking his head.

She stopped and looked at him. "What do you mean? He did great. True, he was a little intimidated by the water at first, but he did great." She paused. "Do you know something that I don't?"

Dylan shrugged. "There's nothing to tell. They've been trying to get Tyson into the water for the past three days," Dylan informed her. "He wouldn't get in for anyone. Whatever you did today was magic. Ask Elena how many times she's tried to get him to swim with her."

"Really? I just asked him to swim with me."

"You've got kid magic," he told her, holding open one of the double doors to the kitchen so they could go get their own meal.

She blushed at the compliment as she passed him. She tucked a strand of wet hair behind her ear and gave him a shy grin that nearly made his knees give out. Good lord, she was stunning. She had no idea the effect she must have on men with that smile.

Not only was she kind, smart, and great with kids, she had a smile that made his mind do happy somersaults, and his body want to follow. It had been a long time since he'd found someone that made him feel all those things at once.

He wanted to ask her out. He wanted to ask her to come back to his place so he could take those wet clothes off her and see the rest of her beauty, but he kept his mouth shut. Not only was that too fast, but she was also on the run from an ex-boyfriend. The last thing in the world she would want is another guy in her life.

Chef turned as they approached and her face fell as she looked at the two of them.

"Oh no. You two haven't eaten yet, have you?" Chef asked.

Bonnie shook her head. "No, but the chicken smells amazing."

Chef's shoulders slumped, and she stepped to the side. Scattered behind her all over the usually clean floor was tonight's chicken dinner. It looked like someone tripped and knocked the container over, spilling it everywhere.

"I don't have any more," Chef said sadly. She shrugged. "I can make you a grilled cheese, but that's all I've got for dinner now."

"It's not a problem, Chef," Dylan assured her, an idea coming to him. "We'll go to Sandy's."

The more he thought about it, the more the chicken falling on the floor was a blessing in disguise. He could take Bonnie out to dinner, without having to actually ask her out. He wanted to find out more about her. He wanted to spend time with her and see her smile again. This was a great option.

"We will?" Bonnie asked, turning to look at him.

"Oh, you should *definitely* go to Sandy's," Chef told her, nodding emphatically. "I make a good burger, but Sandy's is out of this world. And the cheese curds? To die for. Go to Sandy's."

Chef gave Dylan a wink. She'd been trying to set him up with a "nice girl" since he'd shown up on the ranch. He was just glad that Chef had decided that Bonnie was a nice girl. For once, he was glad for her help.

Bonnie looked back and forth between him and Chef. If

she suspected something, she stayed quiet. She shrugged. "Okay. I'll need to change first, though."

"Wear something cute," Chef advised. "It's not fancy, but cute is always good."

Bonnie nodded slowly at her. "Okay."

"I'll meet you outside your cabin in ten minutes," Dylan said. He put his hand on her shoulder and guided her out of the kitchen and away from Chef. He didn't want the motherly woman to get too pushy and scare Bonnie off of dinner.

"Okay. Sounds good." Bonnie flashed him a smile and waved to Chef before heading out of the kitchen to change. Dylan watched the wet spots and knew he was a lucky man.

"Make sure you get her the cheese curds," Chef told him, pointing her wooden spoon at him like an extended finger.

"You know, the saying is 'the fastest way to a *man's* heart is through his stomach'," he teased her.

"It's really a gender-neutral thing," she assured him. "Food makes everyone fall in love. That's why fancy restaurants and date nights exist."

Dylan laughed. "Oh, Chef."

"I'm serious about those cheese curds, though Dylan." Chef pointed her wooden spoon at him. "This one's a keeper."

He looked out the small kitchen window to see her walking through the early evening sunshine, and he had to agree.

I just hope she wants to be kept, he thought to himself.

Chapter 12

BONNIE CHANGED her shirt twice and put on more mascara than usual. She was nervous.

This felt like a date. Only, it totally wasn't. At least she didn't think it was. They were simply going out to a restaurant because the ranch didn't have any food. That was it. He was being a good co-worker. There was nothing romantic about it.

Even though she wanted there to be.

Either way, she was nervous now. It felt enough like a date to make her stomach queasy, and her legs want to move around.

She made sure her hair looked nice enough and that her mascara wasn't leaving raccoon circles under her eyes. She didn't really have enough time to get truly dolled up, so she hoped this would do. She had her favorite pale blue t-shirt that gave her just a little bit of cleavage and her best jeans that she knew made her ass look good.

She nodded to herself in the small mirror and headed out to meet Dylan.

She found him leaning up against a cherry red sports car, looking for all the world like something out of a magazine. He had on jeans and a leather jacket. He looked like sex on a stick, especially leaning up against the car.

"Wow," she said, coming up to look at the car. "Is this yours?"

"Nah, I stole it." She looked up at him, and he laughed. "Is it okay if I drive? Your car is mostly fixed, but I don't trust it yet. I still need to replace a few things."

Gratitude flowed through her. "Thank you so much for doing that. You really don't have to replace stuff. At least let me pay for some of it."

He shrugged and waved her off. "It's actually been fun to work on it. Since Mia's husband Carter owns W Motors, all the cars around here are either in pristine shape or electric. I've loved getting my hands messy in an engine again."

Immediately, Bonnie's mind took the phrase to a dirty place. She would like him to get messy with her engine. If he could make her car purr, she could only imagine what he could do with her body.

"I really appreciate it," she repeated, forcing the sexual thoughts from her mind.

He opened up the passenger-side door for her to get in. If the cherry red sleek exterior was nice, the inside was even better. Everything was smooth lines and leather. It smelled like new car and felt like she was in the most comfortable chair of her life. It was hard to believe this was a car.

"Wow," she whispered, running her hand along the dash. "What kind of car is this?"

"Ferrari," he replied, putting on his seat-belt.

Bonnie's eyes bugged out a little bit. "I've never even seen a real Ferrari. How do you have a Ferrari?"

"I told you," he said with a shrug. "I stole it."

She gave him a stern look as he started the engine. It hummed like a musical instrument. He pumped the gas, making it roar for a second, and she grinned.

"Seriously, how do you have this car?" she asked, looking around. "How does a ranch hand at a non-profit ranch for foster kids afford something like this? I'm guessing Mia doesn't give them out as bonus perks."

He laughed and revved the engine again before pulling out onto the dirt road leading out of the ranch. He went slow, keeping an eye out for kids. Even on the uneven gravel, the car sailed like she was floating.

"I wasn't always a ranch hand," he told her.

"Okay." She smiled at him. He was enjoying having her have to figure him out. "So, what did you do before?"

"I owned a company."

She looked around at the very fancy car. "Must have been some company. Why'd you quit? You must have been good at whatever you did."

"I hated it," he replied, pulling onto the highway. The car sped up, and she fell back in her seat with the momentum of it. She'd never been in a car that accelerated like this. She wondered for a moment if this was what astronauts felt like when they went up into space.

The engine hummed like it was singing with joy as they zipped along the mountain road. She remembered her own engine sounding far less happy.

"I was constantly working," he continued once the car got up to speed. "Yeah, I made a lot of money, but I had no life. I woke up, got on my computer, ate on my computer, worked out on my computer, and then barely slept because I was thinking about my computer. It wasn't living."

"I'm sorry," Bonnie said softly. She thought about reaching out and taking his hand but didn't. She wasn't supposed to get attached to the people here.

"Don't be." He guided the car around a turn without having to slow down. The car took the turn with graceful ease. "I sold my company, and I haven't touched a computer for anything other than emailing my mom. It's fantastic."

"I'm sure your mom appreciates that," she said with a chuckle. She looked at the car again. "What company was it?"

He turned and grinned at her, his dark eyes sparkling. "You really want to know?"

"I do now." Her curiosity piqued. What kind of business could he have had to be able to buy a Ferrari?

"FirmHard Tech." He said it and then waited for her response to the name.

It sounded familiar. She rolled the name on her tongue for a moment before it hit her where she recognized it. Three months ago, the sale was the only the only thing the news seemed capable of talking about.

"You're the owner of FirmHard Tech? The one Google bought for one point three billion dollars?" She remembered the newscasters saying how the company was going to bring in even more money for Google, but that the CEO wasn't part of the purchase price.

"That's me." He grinned at her.

"No way," she said after a moment. "You've got to be kidding me."

"Well, if the Ferrari doesn't do it for you, feel free to look me up." He nodded to her phone in her lap. "Dylan Abbott. Two B's, two T's."

She narrowed her eyes but pulled up the search function on her phone and typed in his name. Immediately a list of news reports with his name and FirmHard Tech popped up. She clicked on the first one that had an image.

It was definitely him. His hair was shorter, and he had on glasses, but it was him.

"No way," she whispered. He laughed.

She held up the photo so she could compare him to it. The face was the same, but he looked older in the photo. He looked tired.

Dylan turned and smiled for her, giving her an even better comparison. There was a light in his eyes now that there wasn't in the picture. He looked happier now. The person was the same, but yet totally different. She much preferred the current happy Dylan to the exhausted one in the picture.

"I can't believe you sold it," she said, putting the phone back in her lap as he turned into a parking lot. "I heard you could have gotten even more."

"It was eating me alive," he told her, pulling into a parking space on the edge of the lot next to a big blue spruce. "I hated my life." His shoulders tensed and the dead look from the picture crept into his face as he remembered. He shook himself, bringing back the smile. "I'm much happier now."

"I'm glad," she told him. "But, if you don't mind me asking, why are you here?"

"I'm here because I'm taking you to dinner," he teased, pointing to the restaurant behind them. She rolled her eyes.

"You're a freaking billionaire," she replied, ignoring his joke. "You could be out on a yacht in Tahiti with female tennis players and lady active-wear models."

"Did that already. I got bored." He shrugged. "It wasn't me. I wasn't happy."

"You weren't happy in Tahiti surrounded by beautiful women catering to your every need?"

He chuckled. "It was fun, don't get me wrong, but there was no life. There were no connections. I wasn't making a difference in the world. I was just spending money and getting sunburned."

"That doesn't sound terrible," she told him.

"It was a great vacation, but it wasn't life." He looked at her with his dark eyes and ran a hand through his messy black hair, ruffling it up at odd ends. "I wanted to find my passion. I'm still looking for it, but at least at the ranch, I'm making a difference. I'm helping people. I have meaning here."

Bonnie thought of her own life. She thought of how good it felt to help Tyson today. To have that passion and reward for making a positive change in the world. A yacht in Tahiti was amazing, but changing a life was forever.

"I can get that," she said slowly. "But, why not just start your own charity? Isn't that what billionaires do?"

"Why not just help a friend's charity that I believe in?" he countered.

"Good point," she conceded. She put on a pair of sunglasses from her purse. She wasn't too worried about anyone recognizing her here, but she wasn't going to be stupid about it either.

He grinned at her and clicked a button, opening up her door for her. She chuckled as he hurried out to offer her his hand to help her out of the low car. It was technology and chivalry all in one.

"A billionaire and a gentleman," she said, taking his

hand in hers. If felt right to touch him. "Two rare creatures. I should go buy a lottery ticket or something."

"Even if you won, I'd still be richer than you," he teased, making her laugh.

He shut the car door behind her before putting his hand on the small of her back and guiding her toward the restaurant. It felt good to have his hand on her. She liked him touching her. Not only did it feel good, but she felt safe.

For the first time in weeks, she wasn't a nervous wreck about being in public. She was still being cautious and watching her surroundings like a hawk, but the anxiety wasn't there. She wasn't scared, just on guard. It was an amazing thing, and it was because Dylan was with her.

Chapter 13

onnie

HE HELD the restaurant door open for Bonnie like a gentleman. She smiled as she passed him, looking around as she entered. Inside, the restaurant was rustic and adorable. Everything appeared to be made of wood, and there was a friendly warmth to the restaurant. While it didn't look like much on the outside, the delicious smell of food inside was enough to make her mouth water.

Dylan waved to the bartender and grabbed a pair of menus from the hostess stand before guiding Bonnie to an empty table. She figured he had to be a regular here. There were several full tables, but still plenty of space for the dinner crowd to come in.

"I highly recommend the green chili burger," Dylan said, handing her a menu once she was seated in her booth. "It's fantastic. Just the right amount of spicy."

She grinned and perused the menu. Her stomach

rumbled. She was hungry after swimming. Everything on the menu looked good, but she was going to go with his personal recommendation.

"Green chili burger it is," she announced. "Oh, and of course these cheese curds."

He raised his eyebrows and set his own menu to the side.

"I heard Chef," she told him with a shrug. "She said they were good and we should have them."

He chuckled. "Yup. The best. They taste as good as the ones in Wisconsin. I think they use the same cheese."

She nodded and perused the menu, just to make sure there wasn't anything else she wanted. It was comfortable sitting with him.

"So, you gave up the good life to come work on a ranch," she said after a moment of quiet between them. "How's it working out for you?"

"Amazing." He smiled, and it lit up the room. His eyes were so brown they were almost black, but when he smiled, they sparkled like precious black diamonds. "At my old job, I couldn't trust anyone. Everyone was fake and out to make a name for themselves at any cost. I wasn't happy."

"And you're happy now?" she asked.

He smiled, and the full weight of his gaze landed on her. "I am."

She wasn't entirely sure if he meant that he was happy here with her or just in general. Either way, it made her feel like she was blushing.

"What can I get you two to drink?" The waiter saved her from having to ask him what he was happy about.

"Just water for me," she said quickly.

"Lemonade for me, please," Dylan told the waiter. He looked at Bonnie. "Get whatever you want. Tonight's my treat."

"I can't," she said shaking her head. She didn't want to take advantage of him. Even knowing he was a billionaire, she didn't want to order more than was necessary. It felt rude.

"I can afford it, I promise," he said with a smile.

She chuckled. "Water, please. With a lemon."

The waiter nodded and wrote down the added lemon on his pad of paper. "Are you two ready to order?"

Dylan looked to check with her, and she nodded, so he told the waiter, "I'll have a green chili burger, medium rare with extra chilies." He looked over at Bonnie and grinned. "And an order of cheese curds."

"I'll have the same," Bonnie told the waiter, handing him the menu. The waiter quickly made a mark on her paper and smiled before heading off to the kitchen.

"I have to ask you something," Dylan said, leaning back in his seat.

"Okay..." Bonnie's shoulders tensed. She wasn't ready to tell him about the Trio. She wasn't ready to tell him what her brother saw. She did her best to keep her face steady, but she glanced over to the exit before she could stop herself.

"How did you get Tyson into the water so easily?" he asked. Bonnie let out a small breath. "Elena's practically had to force him to just put his feet in the water. You had him splashing and halfway to actually swimming in thirty minutes. How'd you do it?"

"I've done it before," she admitted. "I'm a kindergarten teacher. And I used to give swim lessons."

"I remember you saying that," he replied, looking interested.

Her chest tightened as she remembered that she wasn't a teacher anymore. She was on the run. Her brother was a material witness, and she was the threat to get him not to testify.

"I mean, I was," she said, trying to push the hurt away. "I was a special ed teacher. I worked primarily with autism and sensory kids at my school."

"I've heard of autism, but not sensory kids," he said. "What's that?"

"Sensory Processing disorder is very common in kids with autism, but shows up in lots of other kids too. Basically, their brains don't process sensory information correctly. So, normal sensations, like a scratchy t-shirt tag or a fire engine passing by, are far too intense and can even be painful," she explained. "Or, the reverse can be true, and they aren't getting enough sensory info. So, those kids tend to always be moving and searching for more stimulation."

"Wow." He thought about it for a moment, digesting her words. "How do you teach someone to deal with that?"

"That's where therapy comes into play," she told him. "A lot of what we did in my classroom was working on making the overwhelming sensations less scary. If we could make them fun, that was always the best."

"Give me an example," he requested.

She thought for a second. "We play with stuff. I like to make sensory bins where kids can squish and experience sensations. I fill bins with spaghetti, pudding, jello, sand, beads, beans, water beads, and anything else I can think of. Then we just play and make the sensations fun."

"A tub of jello sounds like fun to me," he agreed. "Do you have any ideas for Tyson?"

She grinned. "I do." This was the part of her job that she loved. She loved figuring out what would help an individual child get past a fear. "I'd love to get some water stuff for him. Things like squirt guns and water balloons. Anything that gets him wet and makes water a fun and pleasant sensation. He doesn't like the way water feels on his face, so the goal would be to make it so much fun that it's no longer unpleasant to be wet."

"Does it work?" Dylan asked.

"Depends on the kid," she admitted. "Each kid needs a different approach, and it takes time. It's important to remember that their behaviors aren't naughty or bad. They're just overwhelmed. It's hard to un-overwhelm."

Dylan smiled. "You must love your work."

She crinkled her brow but smiled. "Why do you say that?"

"You light up when you talk about this," he told her. "You're practically glowing, and your whole body is animated."

Her cheeks instantly heated and she folded her hands on the table.

Dylan reached across the table. "It's a good thing," he said. "It's beautiful. I'm sorry your ex took it away from you."

"My ex?" Bonnie repeated confused. She caught herself before blowing her story. "Oh, right. My ex."

She shrugged and quickly tried to think of something to say to make it less awkward. Luckily, the waiter returned then with their drinks. She gulped at her water, grateful for the interruption.

"I guess that you're pretty over him," Dylan said, taking a small sip of his lemonade.

She inhaled and took in a lungful of water. She started coughing and sputtering. "What?"

"Your ex," he repeated. "You sound over him."

"Right. Right, my ex." She cleared her throat and set her glass down. "We were officially over when things went south. I thought we'd moved on."

She'd rehearsed this lie several times, but she hated telling it to Dylan. She didn't want to lie to him. She wanted to tell him everything, but she didn't want to put him in that position either. It wasn't fair to drag him into her issues with *them*.

"What happened?" he asked, genuine concern in his voice. It made her guilt deepen.

"We broke up. Then, a few weeks ago, I came home and found my house on fire," she told him. It was sort of close to the truth. She tried to keep her story as close to the truth as possible. It made her less likely to slip up.

"Did you go to the police?" he asked, his dark eyes concerned for her.

"Of course, but there was no definitive proof that I was in danger," she explained. She remembered her nightmare. "The fire investigator said that I left my book on the stove and it caught fire. It happens."

"Did you leave a book?" he asked.

"I'd never seen the book before," she explained. "It was called, *'You're Next.'* They also found the remains of the rest of the series in the kitchen. Their titles were *'Dead Man Walking'* and *'Dead and Deader.'* They weren't my books."

"He put them there?" he asked. "That's a heck of a warning."

"Yeah," she agreed. "So I ran. I know that he's out there. I think I'm safe for now. I've crossed state lines, and I don't think he has a good way to track me, but..."

She shrugged. She hoped *they* weren't tracking her. She hoped that they still had the wrong last name for her. She knew her files were being monitored by the police. She would hopefully get some warning if they accessed anything the police had marked. But that wasn't something she had control over. Anxiety crept up in her chest.

She needed to change the subject.

"So, is this the main restaurant in town, or are there others I need to try?" she asked with a smile.

He took her hint and let the subject drop. "This is basically it for Silver Springs," he replied. "There's a grocery store nearby, but if you want more than that, you have to go to the next town over. Evergreen has a Walmart *and* a Walgreen's."

"Wow, that sounds like the place to be," she told him. He grinned.

"Sandy's is still better than anything they have there," he assured her. "I promise."

She grinned. "Well, hopefully, our food comes soon to prove it," she said. "I'm hungry."

"Speak of the devil." He nodded behind her at the server returning with two plates piled high with food. The spicy smell of the chilies made her mouth instantly start to water.

She was barely able to wait until they both had their plates in front of them before taking a bite. He watched as she brought the burger to her mouth and took a bite.

It was just as good and even better than he promised. She moaned, and he grinned before taking a bite of his own dinner.

Chapter 14

DYLAN WALKED Bonnie to the door of her cabin, sad that the night was already ending. She paused at the door and flashed him a huge smile before disappearing inside. He smiled and waved before turning to head back.

The sky was bright with stars. The afternoon storms had been short today, and now the sky was clear and full of tiny lights as he walked back to his car.

He had butterflies in his stomach. They were dancing around with excitement from being around her all evening. He couldn't believe how long they'd talked. The two of them had shut Sandy's down. He watched as the light in her room flickered on. He liked knowing that she was safe.

He had been worried that the ex-boyfriend was going to be a problem. He'd been worried that she was going to be still hung up on the guy, but that didn't seem to be the case.

She seemed barely able to remember him, other than the fact that he was out to get her.

That was a good sign if he wanted to ask her out on a real date. He was going to do it, and just the thought made him nervous and happy at the same time.

She made him feel light. When she smiled, he wanted to smile too. When she spoke about her passion for kids and helping them with their needs, he wanted to help them too. She made him want to do more.

She was a perfect fit for the ranch. Mia had been right to hire her. Her experience with special needs kids would be incredibly helpful at the ranch. There were so many kids in the system that needed a little bit more help, and she would be able to do that here. It felt almost like fate.

He hoped she was going to stay. He could tell himself it was because she was good for the ranch, but really he wanted her to stay because she was good for him.

He opened the car door, and a drop of water from the big pine tree sprinkled onto his cheek. He wiped at it absentmindedly, but the water on his face made him think of Tyson and what she'd said at dinner.

An idea formed in his head. She said to do something fun, so that was exactly what he was going to do. He grinned and hopped into his car and drove quickly to the garage. He had things to do before morning.

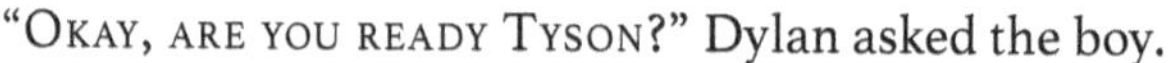

"Okay, are you ready Tyson?" Dylan asked the boy.

Tyson stood before him in his swim trunks and a rash-guard shirt that was a little too big for him, but a smile plastered across his face. Dylan couldn't help but like the kid.

"Do you think she'll be excited?" Tyson asked. His smile faltered slightly. "I don't want her to get mad."

Dylan put his hand on the kid's shoulder and gave him a gentle squeeze. He thought of what Bonnie had said the night before. "No, she won't be mad as long as you're having fun. Follow me."

Tyson nodded and carefully tiptoed behind Dylan as they circled around the pool shed in the direction of Bonnie's cabin. She would be coming out any moment, and they had to be ready.

They hid in the shadow of the shed as she approached. She had on a bright blue full piece swimsuit with her gray sweats from the day before. The suit accentuated the soft curves of her hips and bust, and he found his mouth going dry. He was glad to see she didn't bring a jacket today and just had her towel wrapped around her shoulders.

He stepped out of the shadow, leaving Tyson ready for their surprise.

"Hi, Dylan," she greeted him with a smile. He loved the way she said his name. "You're coming to the swim lesson, right?"

"I am. You don't have anything on you that can't get wet, do you?" he asked.

She frowned and shook her head. "No. Why?"

"No reason." He handed her a small squirt gun he had hidden behind his back. "You may want this."

She took it, looking completely baffled. "A squirt gun? What..."

That was when all the kids came out. Tyson and most of the other kids at camp all emerged with squirt guns and began an all-out epic water battle.

Dylan had planned it all. It was a water free-for-all. He had large plastic storage bins full of water balloons and filled squirt guns placed around the pool area. He'd gotten all the camp hoses and had them spraying sprinkler style to create a water playground for the kids to run through as they squirted and threw balloons at one another.

The air around the pool filled with the sounds of water and shrieks of laughter. He looked over at Bonnie and for a split second was terrified he'd done something wrong. But, then her beautiful brown eyes lit up. She dropped her swim towel and aimed her gun directly at his chest, letting out a long stream of water and drenching him. With a laugh, she then ran to squirt Tyson next.

He tried to follow but was ambushed by a group of kids with squirt guns. He emerged a few moments later, completely soaked and his squirt gun empty. He needed to reload and get back into the fight. Out of the corner of his eye, he saw Bonnie trying to sneak up on Tyson to get him with her squirt gun.

Dylan ran to the nearest bin of water balloons as and threw one at Tyson. The kid ducked, and the balloon sailed over Tyson's head and landed squarely in on Bonnie's chest. She narrowed her eyes and ran at him, with her gun pointed directly at him once again. She squirted him until her gun ran out.

He grabbed her hand and pulled her to where he had several loaded squirt guns ready to go. They each grabbed one, and he made sure to squirt her before she could get him this time. She laughed as the water splattered against her swimsuit.

Dylan couldn't remember the last time he'd had this much fun. He was laughing so hard his chest hurt, and he was fairly sure his face would be frozen into a smile for the rest of his life.

A water balloon smacked square into his chest. If his

shirt wasn't already drenched, he certainly was now. He looked up to find the attacker and saw Tyson reach for a second water balloon. But, Dylan didn't care about the balloon.

He cared that Tyson was soaking wet. His hair was drenched, and water was streaming down his cheeks. And the best part was that Tyson was having so much fun, he didn't care. Dylan found Bonnie grinning as she noticed the same thing. Their eyes met, and she smiled.

She gave him a thumbs up, and her eyes told him he'd done a good job.

Dylan had been having an amazing time, but her smile sent him to the moon with joy.

Chapter 15

onnie

"THAT WAS AMAZING," Bonnie declared. She couldn't wipe the grin off her face, despite the fact the water fight had ended fifteen minutes earlier. "I can't believe you organized all this in one night."

She motioned around the pool area. It was a disaster now, but she was impressed with everything he'd set up. There were empty squirt guns laying haphazardly on the ground. They mixed with broken balloon pieces in the grass. She bent down to pick up a discarded squirt gun and put it in a bucket she carried on her arm.

"Every once in a while I have a good idea," Dylan told her, picking up a gun and putting it in the tub he held at his hip. He winked at her, making her grin.

"This was beyond brilliant," she told him. "Did you see how much Tyson enjoyed it? He didn't even realize his hair was wet, and even when he did, he was having so much fun he didn't want to stop."

"He was having a blast. I'm really getting to like the little guy," Dylan agreed, picking up another squirt gun. He still wore his wet swim trunks, and his gray t-shirt hugged his chest and abs like a second skin. She was just as wet in her own swimsuit and soaked sweatpants.

"This was fantastic. I had a lot of fun," she told him. She wished she had better words to describe how happy the water fight had made her, but she couldn't seem to find them. "Thank you."

He grinned at her. His smile made her feel tipsy when he looked at her like that. It made her think that he knew how she felt. That he knew she was happy.

"I think we should bring some of these to our swim lesson tomorrow," she said, shifting the nearly full bucket full of squirt guns to her other arm. "I think it would make the lesson even more fun."

"That sounds great," he agreed. He looked around. "I think we've gotten all of them."

She looked around the pool area. Most of the kids had helped pick up the squirt guns before running off to dinner, and it did look like she and Dylan had found most of the guns that didn't make it into the bins. One of the ranch hands was carefully sweeping up the balloon pieces that were on the concrete by the pool with a broom.

"And you're sure the balloons are okay to leave out?" she asked, looking at all the brightly colored pieces in the grass.

"Yes," he assured her as they walked to the pool shed. "They're biodegradable. They'll be gone by tomorrow morning."

"That would have been so nice when we were kids," she

remarked, remembering her parents making her pick up all the tiny latex pieces of summer fun.

He opened the pool shed, and together they walked inside to add their squirt guns to the pile inside. He set his bin down in the corner next to the others before taking her bucket and adding it to the pile.

"Would you be interested in some dinner?" he asked nonchalantly as he organized the plastic weapons.

"I could go for some," she replied. She thought of her green chili burger from the night before, and her stomach grumbled, betraying her hunger.

"Are you thinking about Sandy's burgers?" he asked with a chuckle.

"How did you know?" she asked. She didn't think her stomach was *that* loud.

"Your face got all far away and dreamlike," he replied. He smiled at her. "Most people get that way when they think of Sandy's burgers."

"You got me." She shrugged and smiled. "They're just so good."

He nodded in agreement, and she turned to exit the small pool shed. She pushed open the wooden door of the shed and stopped short. She stood in awe, caught full blast in the beauty of the mountains in front of her.

She stood in the doorway taking them in. The green of the pine trees, the perfect blue of the sky, the brown and purple of the mountains with just the tips of white. Standing there, she finally understood the "America the Beautiful" lyric of "purple mountain majesty."

"They're beautiful, aren't they?" Dylan's voice was soft behind her shoulder. He was close enough to touch her if he wanted and she found herself wanting him to do so.

"Sorry, I didn't mean to trap you in there," she said

quickly, stepping out and turning to the side to let him out. But he didn't move. He stood there, looking at her.

He was so handsome in the late afternoon sunlight. It accented the strength of his jaw and the line of his nose while softening his dark eyes with warmth. Droplets of water from their squirt gun fight glimmered in his dark hair and dripped down the back of his neck.

His eyes met hers, and she swore her heart stopped. Deep pools of rich brown enveloped her and warmth spread through her entire body. He moved toward her, tipping his chin and angling his body into hers. She forgot how to breathe as she realized he was going to kiss her.

Oh good lord did she want him to kiss her. She took a step forward, her hands trembling in anticipation. If this were a movie, there would be swelling romantic music right now.

But, then he paused, catching himself before he touched her. He cleared his throat and looked away as if he had thought better of what he was doing. He stepped back into the shed, shadows falling across his face and hiding his eyes.

"I need to change before dinner," he said quickly. "I'll meet you at your place.

"Um, sure," she stammered, unsure of what was happening. Had she misread him? Her arms wrapped around her middle. She put on a smile she knew didn't reach her eyes. "See you in a few minutes."

Stupidity and embarrassment flowed through her in hot, heavy strokes. She shook her head as she hurried to her cabin. Why would he want to kiss her? He was gorgeous. And a billionaire.

She was a woman on the run with messy hair.

She turned before she could make a bigger fool of herself and saw a teenager staring at them. He was probably around sixteen. She recognized him as one of the younger camp counselors. He often worked with Elena, and she knew the two of them were close. He walked over to her.

"I found this." He held out a squirt gun from the earlier fight. "I thought I'd put it away."

"Thanks."

"No problem." The teen smiled at her and turned to leave. She felt like an idiot. No wonder Dylan didn't kiss her. They had an audience.

She took the squirt gun back to the shed and handed it to Dylan. He took it without a word.

"See you in a little bit," she said lamely, and she quickly turned to walk to her cabin. The moment was gone.

She walked quickly. She wanted that kiss, but she knew it wasn't happening. She just had terrible luck. She told herself it was probably for the best.

Sure, they had fun together. He certainly made her laugh, and he was funny and smart. They'd had a great time at dinner the night before. However, she was on the run. If the police called, if a strange car showed up, if she saw something odd, she would have to run. It was better not to get attached, no matter how good looking he was.

She opened the door to her cabin and went inside to change, muttering to herself that she needed to get a grip.

She rinsed off in the bathroom and quickly changed into jeans and a cute t-shirt. It was a good thing there wasn't a dress code at the camp or at Sandy's because she had nothing else to wear. Since the fire burned most of her clothing, she'd been living out of a suitcase. She'd packed a few things, but she'd never intended to only have three outfits. The suitcase was supposed to be a temporary thing, not her long-term wardrobe.

She wished she had something to put on that wasn't

jeans and a t-shirt. She wished she could look cute tonight. It would certainly help her mood.

She ran a brush through her hair and decided she would pick out some new clothes online. She was finally someplace she could stay long enough to deal with shipping. A few new shirts and maybe a skirt or dress would make her feel prettier.

She sighed and headed out to meet him. She still felt like an idiot, but she was hungry, and they were getting dinner. He was still the closest thing she had to a friend here. She didn't want to be alone just because she was on the run. It was just her luck she's meet a great guy when she had to hide from the mob.

She stepped out onto the porch of the cabin and took in a deep breath. He wasn't here yet. There wasn't a thunderstorm today, which she was glad of. The sun was starting to creep closer to the mountains for the night, and the scent of pine was thick in the air. It always amazed her how late the sun set in the summer.

She stepped off the porch and saw him walking toward her. Her body heated as she looked at him. He had on his faded jeans, low-slung and ripped at the knee and t-shirt that fit him perfectly. Somehow still looked like he just walked off the catwalk. She had a hard time believing that this guy had sat behind a desk to make his living. His broad shoulders and trim waist made it look like he'd worked on cars and with his hands his whole life instead.

"All ready?" he asked. He stopped short of her with a friendly smile.

Friends, she told herself. *Just friends.* He had seemed to have completely forgotten their almost kiss earlier if it hadn't been all in her mind in the first place. Maybe she was just hallucinating due to hunger.

"Yup," she said, putting on a smile of her own. "I'm ready for that hamburger."

This time he'd left his car in the garage, so they walked across the ranch. She made sure to keep her distance and not accidentally bump her hand into his. Even though she wanted to. The last thing she wanted was for him to stop spending time with her because she tried too hard to kiss him.

THE CAR RIDE down to Sandy's was comfortable, and she started to relax. He liked alternative rock on the radio, and they talked about music. She preferred country, and he only teased her a little bit about it before turning on a country station.

"Wow, the place looks packed," Bonnie said as they pulled into the parking lot. Every spot seemed to have a car in it. Dylan pulled around to the back and managed to find a spot just as someone was leaving.

"It'll be fine," Dylan promised, but he didn't sound terribly confident about it.

They got out of the car and walked into the restaurant. The night before, they'd walked in and sat right down, but tonight they could barely get in the entrance.

"Do you want to wait?" Bonnie asked as someone jostled her shoulder. Being in the crowd made her nervous. She didn't like crowds since it was too hard to see if someone was watching her. "Maybe we could go someplace else?"

"No," he said firmly. "Green chili burger, right?"

She nodded, keeping her arms wrapped around her.

"I'll be right back," he told her. He touched her shoulder gently, but it didn't put her at ease. She put her back to the wall so she could watch everyone else. She wasn't hungry anymore. Not with this many people around. The space between her shoulder blades itched like someone was watching her.

She knew it was silly. No one knew she was in town here. No one was even paying attention to her, but she still felt like she was wearing a neon sign with an arrow pointing to her for the mob to see.

Dylan made his way to the bar. She recognized the bartender as Elena. Her long dark hair was pulled back into a ponytail. Dylan said something to her, and she looked up, meeting Bonnie's gaze. She smiled and waved. Bonnie did her best to return the motion. She hoped it looked friendly enough.

Dylan said something more to Elena before making his way back through the crowd to get to her.

"Elena says she can get us the burgers to go in ten minutes," he said, leaning over and speaking quietly into her ear so the other patrons wouldn't hear. She liked how it felt intimate, even if it wasn't.

"Seriously?" Bonnie pulled back and looked around. The place was packed. Ten minutes was barely long enough to get the food cooked, let alone cook it with all the orders the restaurant had to be receiving.

"There are perks to having someone on the inside," he told her. "I have friends in high places. I don't know if you know this, but I'm kind of a big deal."

She raised her eyebrows at him. "I'm sure you are."

"I'm basically a king in Silver Springs," he replied, brushing his shoulder in an exaggerated motion as he puffed out his chest. He winked at her.

She laughed, feeling a little more at ease with him near her. "Or Elena is just awesome."

"That's possible too," he agreed with a smile. "Can I get you a drink? I happen to know someone."

She thought about it. A drink sounded great, but ever since the fire, she didn't like the way alcohol made her feel. She needed to stay sharp and in control. "I'm good. Thanks."

"Okay." He shrugged and leaned against the wall next to her.

It was hardly three minutes before Elena reappeared at the bar and held up a large paper bag. Dylan touched Bonnie's shoulder with a smile before heading through the crowd to pick it up. Bonnie hesitated for half a second before following him.

"Thank you for calling in your order, Mr. Abbott," Elena announced. She winked at Dylan as she handed him the bag.

"Thanks, Elena," he replied, handing her a couple of crisp bills. "See you later."

"No problem." Elena waved to Bonnie before going back to serving drinks to the people at the bar.

Dylan led the way through the crowd to the front door with Bonnie right behind him. She was glad they were leaving the restaurant. The crowd and the noise had her nerves on high alert. She was actually glad they weren't getting a table because she wasn't sure she could have eaten comfortably in there with that many people.

Outside, the air felt crisp and clean. She took a deep breath in and felt less like throwing up. She wished she didn't have to feel so afraid all the time. After the trial, she told herself, everything could go back to the way it was before.

"I know a great place we can go to eat this," Dylan said, holding up the bag of food. "It'll take just a couple of minutes to get there."

"Okay," Bonnie agreed. They were halfway to the car when Bonnie realized he'd paid for her meal yet again. "You didn't have to pay again, you know. I should pay you back."

He shrugged. "I can afford it. Promise."

She crossed her arms. "No."

He turned and looked at her. "Okay." He smiled as if he were pleasantly surprised at her insistence. "Next time is on you. Sound good?"

She nodded curtly. "Yes."

He chuckled and opened up her door for her. She slid inside, and he handed her the food. She put on her seat belt as he got in and started the car. The food smelled so good it had her mouth watering before they'd even left the parking lot.

Chapter 16

DYLAN REVVED the engine and headed out on the main highway before turning off onto a small side road. It was one of his favorite places to watch the sunset. He hoped Bonnie would enjoy it. The sports car didn't struggle to speed up the big hill even a little bit. Dylan was fairly certain he would be pushing her car at this point. He still needed to put in the new equipment he'd ordered for her.

The road curved and wound its way through pine trees and aspen. They passed some large houses before coming to an open space where he pulled off to the side of the road.

"Here we are," he announced, putting the car in park and stepping out.

He quickly went over and opened her car door, barely making it before she opened it herself. He enjoyed being a gentleman. She smiled as she got out of the car, even though she shook her head a little. She was her own woman.

Her eyes went wide as she saw where he had brought her.

The view was amazing. Spectacular, actually.

There was a wooden bench that sat perched on the edge of a cliff. The cliff gave way to a valley that then turned into the Rocky Mountains. He loved to sit here and contemplate the ancient peaks. It was always quiet and beautiful here, and he'd timed the sunset perfectly.

The sun blazed its final glory behind the tallest peak as it settled in for the night. The color was breathtaking. Orange and blue clouds filled the sky and reflected off the mountain peaks. Everything was bathed in color and light.

"It's a Bronco sunset," Dylan remarked. He stood next to her, looking out at the view.

"A what?" Bonnie asked, confused. She didn't look at him but rather continued to stare at the sky.

"A Bronco sunset," Dylan repeated. "The Denver Broncos are the football team here. Their colors are orange and blue. When the sky is like this, the locals say that it proves God is a Bronco fan."

She looked out at the blue sky and the orange sunset. "I'm certainly a fan now."

He chuckled and held up the bag of food. She'd forgotten it in the car, but he hadn't. "Hungry?"

"Yeah. Sorry," she said. He loved the soft blush that flattered her cheeks. She moved to the bench so they could sit and eat.

"Don't be. You were looking at the scenery." He pulled out a neatly wrapped burger and handed it to her before pulling out a container of food for himself.

"What did you get?" she asked, peeling back the paper and taking a bite of her burger. She groaned a little with pleasure. The sound went straight to his groin, and he had to concentrate on his food instead of her.

"Jambalaya," he said, taking off the lid and showing her the inside. The spicy scent of the mixture of rice, shrimp, and sausage made his stomach growl. He was hungrier than he thought. "Want some?"

"Um, sure," she said. He handed her his fork, and she took a small bite. She made that noise again, and he had to think of baseball stats. "Oh, that's spicy. But definitely good."

He nodded. "I know, right? Sandy's is the only place out here that I've found that even gets close to the real thing."

"Did you grow up in the south?" she asked, taking a bite of her burger.

He shook his head. "No. But, my grandfather is from New Orleans, so we used to go every summer when I was a kid. He made the best jambalaya I've ever had."

He smiled, thinking of his grandfather. Those summer trips were some of his favorite times.

"Sounds like a good memory," she said, watching him as he took a bite of his food. "Do you ever go back?"

He nodded as he ate. It tasted like home. "I try and go once a year. It's a great city."

"I've never been," she said.

"Really?"

She shook her head. "My parents moved all over the place when my brother and I were kids, but it was mostly in the Midwest and then the East coast. My dad was a salesman."

"My dad was an electrician," Dylan said. "Then a farmer once he met my mom. But, he loved automating the farm for her."

"Makes sense that you got into computers then," she

replied. "My mom was a nurse. I think I got the helper gene from her."

Together they ate their meal, watching the sunset. As the sun dipped lower, the colors of the sky became more vivid and colorful. Dylan wasn't sure he'd ever seen such deep oranges and such vibrant blues in the sky before.

"Where did you grow up?" Bonnie asked after a quiet moment. "I'm guessing not New Orleans since you said you went there to visit."

"Kansas," he replied. "It's where my mother's side of the family lives. My sister's still out there. She married a farmer. She calls me the black sheep of the family since I didn't go into farming."

She looked over at him, her warm brown eyes taking him in. He liked the way she looked at him and wished again he could kiss her. He had almost done so earlier, but they'd been interrupted. He wanted it to be memorable since he had a feeling he'd never have another first kiss again after kissing her. He didn't want another first kiss. Just her kisses.

"You could have been a farmer," she told him. "You certainly work hard enough."

He chuckled. "My dad used to say I got my mechanical brain from him, but that I got my work ethic from my mom's side."

She smiled. "He must be very proud of you."

Heartache hit his chest. He looked out at the mountains and sighed. "He died just before I sold my company. He was proud of me even though he didn't know exactly what I had made."

She put her hand on his knee. Heat rose at her touch. "I'm so sorry, Dylan."

"His death was actually a big part of why I sold Firm-

Hard Tech," he explained. Guilt wound in his stomach. "I was so busy. I knew he was sick, but I was working. I didn't have time to visit him, even when we knew it was the end. I had to work. I was working in the backseat as they drove me to his funeral."

He could still see his sister shaking her head at him. He could hear his mother asking him to come and stay before his dad went to the hospital. He said he was too busy. He was always too busy. And for what? His company didn't save the world. It simply made tech companies more money.

"You miss him," Bonnie said quietly. "I'm so sorry, Dylan."

"Thank you." He still wasn't sure how to respond when people said that. Her hand was still on his knee. He put his own hand on top of hers. Her hand was small beneath his, and he never wanted to let go. "What about you? Do you have any family?"

"My parents are currently touring Europe," she replied, letting him change the subject. "My brother... um, well, he's in security. He's figuring things out, but he's really smart."

"I'm guessing he's younger," Dylan said. He recognized the way he talked about his sister. She smiled as she spoke of him.

She grinned. "Yup. He's always getting into trouble. He's got a good heart, though. I think you'd like him."

"If he's like you, I'm sure I would," Dylan replied. He liked that she flushed at the compliment.

"So, do you bring girls up here all the time?" she asked coyly. She pointed to the view of the mountains. The sun was almost set, but the sky was still filled with swirls of gold, orange, blues, and purples. "It seems like a great way to make an impression."

"Are you impressed?" he asked. She still had her hand on his knee.

"Maybe a little," she replied with a smile.

Her lips were perfect. He wanted to feel the shape of her lips under his own. To taste her sweetness. He knew she would be sweet. He could feel it in his bones that her kisses would be the sweetest kiss he'd ever known.

There were no people here. There was no one to walk by and disturb them this time. He had wanted to kiss her all day. He had nearly kissed her in the shed, but he didn't want her to get in trouble with Mia for kissing on the job.

But here, she could be his.

He reached out and cupped the back of her neck in his hand. Her skin was so soft. He loved the way her breath caught as he touched her. The sunlight gleamed in her hair, bringing out the golden highlights in the dark waves.

Their mouths met, and he was right about her sweetness. Her lips parted, a tease of tongue and teeth, and the lovely liquid weight in his belly increased. The warmth of her kiss heated him straight to the core. Primal desire flooded through him, but he kept himself in check. He wanted to do this right with her.

"Wow," she whispered as he drew back from the kiss. Her eyelashes flickered on her cheek as she kept her eyes closed. When she opened them, he could see the world in her eyes, and it was beautiful. *Wow* indeed.

She bit her bottom lip and smiled at him. "I liked that," she told him softly.

So, he leaned forward and did it again. It was as good as the first time, if not better. This time she flicked her tongue against his lips, taking his taste for her own. Heat coiled in his belly for more than just a kiss.

He pulled back, and she smiled at him again, making his

heart thump in his chest. His attraction to her was so much more than physical. It wasn't just the kiss that had him wanting more. It was her. Her smile, her conversation, her desire to help others. He wanted all of her.

She shivered, and he realized the sun was gone. The sky was dark as stars came out and twinkled in the twilight. At this elevation, once the sun disappeared, it got cold fast, and she didn't have a jacket.

"Let's get you to the car," he said, rising from the bench and offering her his hand. She took it, making his stomach do the happy flip-flop again.

She held his hand all the way to the car and the entire way home. He wanted to take this slow. He wanted to make this feeling last. The tension between them was sweet and yet so delicate. He didn't want to rush this and fall into bed and find they'd gone too quickly.

He wanted to woo her. He wanted to take care of her and make her his forever. Immediate gratification was always good, but this had the potential to be so much more. He wanted it to be so much more.

He dropped her off at her cabin. Part of him hoped she'd ask him inside to continue what they'd started. To be honest, most of him hoped for that. She didn't though. She simply leaned over in her chair and kissed his cheek.

"Thank you." Her voice was soft. "Will I see you tomorrow?"

His voice came out husky. "Yes. Most certainly."

She grinned and bit her bottom lip again as she smiled and got out of the car

He watched as she went to her door, pausing before going in to smile at him.

Yes, he thought to himself as he watched her and felt his heart pound in his chest. *She was worth taking it slow.*

Chapter 17

"Thank you, Tyson." Bonnie took the new roll of paper towels from him with a smile.

"You're welcome, Bonnie," the boy replied. He flashed her a shy smile, his brown eyes happy. "I really liked today."

She gave his shoulder a gentle squeeze. "I thought you might. Was it worth missing our swim lesson for?"

Tyson nodded enthusiastically. "Definitely."

He looked over at the table where his creation lay drying. Bonnie had set up pudding painting for any kids who were interested. She'd been surprised at the amount of kids that had opted to give up their free time before bed to do an art project. Granted, it was painting with pudding, so it was art and a snack.

It was just Tyson and Bonnie now. He'd wanted to stay and help her clean up before getting ready for bed. She appreciated the company and loved the way he smiled at her. He was a great kid.

"Is Dylan going to be at our swim lesson tomorrow?" Tyson asked. "I know he's helping Ms. Laura do something for the horses tonight. But what about tomorrow?"

"I think so," she replied. "He wanted to come paint with us, but Ms. Laura needed his help to take one of the horses into town. I'm sure he'll come tomorrow."

She had hoped to see him today, but an emergency with one of the horses had kept him busy. She wanted to kiss him again. She wanted to talk to him and make sure that last night wasn't just a fluke. She liked him and not getting to eat dinner tonight with him had been strange. At least Tyson had kept her company.

"Okay. Good. I really like having him around," Tyson said with a smile. "What else can I do?"

She smiled at him. He was such a good helper. "We need to bring those empty bowls back to the kitchen," she told him.

"I can do that," he announced. He carefully picked up a stack of empty pudding bowls and balanced them in his hands as he walked to the kitchen. His little tongue stuck out as he concentrated on what he was doing.

She smiled at him as he worked hard not to spill the bowls. She'd made sure to spend some extra time with him today, and it was obvious that the attention was appreciated. He was smiling and had even tried a new food at dinner. She was excited to see what a little more work with him could accomplish. He was such a great kid.

She looked around the room, making sure they had cleaned up the cafeteria after their pudding painting. The only thing left in the room was the picture Tyson had painted. She went over and picked it up.

It was three stick figures. There was a tall stick figure on one side, a small figure in the middle, and a figure wearing what Bonnie assumed was a skirt. They were all holding hands inside a blue square. Tyson said it was a picture of Dylan, Bonnie, and him swimming. It warmed her heart and made it ache at the same time.

She always got attached to her students. It was impossible not to, but Tyson was quickly stealing her heart. She shook her head and set the picture down. She was happy here, just like he was. In the two weeks she'd been here, this felt almost more like home than her townhouse did.

"Bonnie?" Tyson called from the kitchen doors. "There's a stranger asking for you on the back porch."

Bonnie's ice ran cold. All the happy feelings from pudding painting fell from her like dropped water.

"What?"

"It's a man. He says he's looking for you," Tyson told her. He came out of the kitchen and walked toward her. "I don't know him."

She swallowed hard on a suddenly dry throat.

"Did you tell him I was here?" she asked, trying to keep her voice light. She didn't want to scare him.

Tyson nodded proudly. "I said I'd come find you."

Her heart pounded an odd rhythm in her chest. They'd found her. She glanced around, trying to figure out the quickest way out of the building. She needed to make sure Tyson stayed safe. She could drop him off at the kid cabins if she went out the south door. From there, she had her go bag ready. If she could get to her car, she could maybe make it out.

"Bonnie?" Chef stepped through the kitchen doors and smiled at her. "There you are. You have a package."

Bonnie nearly ran right there. She nearly grabbed Tyson

and sprinted, but she noticed the brown box in Chef's hands.

"What?"

"You got a package. It looks like it's from Amazon," Chef said. "I signed for it. The delivery guy just needed a signature."

Bonnie heard a car engine start up and saw the distinctive design of the delivery truck pass outside the window. It was a false alarm.

"Are you okay, Bonnie?" Chef asked, coming over and putting the back of her hand on Bonnie's forehead. "You look like you might be sick."

Bonnie pulled away. "I'm fine. My package wasn't supposed to arrive until tomorrow. It's something for my computer."

Chef handed her the small brown box. "Are you sure you're okay?"

"I'm fine," Bonnie replied automatically. She still wasn't sure that she wasn't going to puke all over the cafeteria floor, but she wasn't going to tell Chef that. "Thank you for the package."

"Sure thing," Chef replied. She frowned but went back to the kitchen to finish prepping food for the next day.

Bonnie needed to be more careful. She didn't realize how unprepared she was until just this minute. What if it hadn't been a delivery? What if they had found her? They would have her, and probably Tyson and Chef too.

"Tyson? I need to go make a phone call. Can you head over to story time?"

"Sure, Bonnie." The boy came over and gave her a big hug. She held him tight for a moment, thanking her lucky stars that the boy was still safe. She needed to protect him. She doubted the Trio would do anything to the staff here, but they could get caught in the crossfire if they came for her.

She made sure he made it safely out to the campfire area where the camp counselors were reading stories to the kids in pajamas. Tyson waved to her before running over to sit next to Elena. She watched him for a second before turning and going back to her cabin.

The camp was quiet all around her as she stood on her porch. The big pines rustled in the wind, but there was no other noise. She could smell rain on the way. She took a deep breath and pulled out her phone. It was a burner phone she'd picked up at a gas station on the state border.

She dialed Detective Patton's number.

"Patton," the familiar voice answered.

"It's Bonnie," she replied, knowing that he wouldn't recognize the number.

"Bonnie! Are you okay?" he asked, but his tone was light. "Are you safe?"

"I'm okay." She took a breath. "Actually, I'm calling you to make sure everything is still okay. How's my brother?"

"He's great," Detective Patton said. She could hear the smile in his voice, and she imagined him sitting at his desk at the police station. "I think he's actually enjoying this. He keeps talking about a job in law enforcement just so he can keep this job up."

She couldn't help but chuckle. Of course, her brother would find a way to make the situation more fun. That was Brett.

"What about me?" She tried to keep her voice even. "Have you heard anything from them? Any threats?"

"There hasn't been anything," he assured her. "It's been quiet. There haven't been any threats to your brother or you.

Whatever you're doing, you're doing a good job of staying quiet. There's no chatter."

"And nothing's popped up on the computer stuff?" she asked, still unconvinced of her safety. She was still spooked.

"I saw your background check request went through last week, but I handled it personally. No one saw it, but me and I made sure nothing could be traced back to you. You're safe on that front. Congrats on the new job, by the way."

She nodded, even though he couldn't see her.

"Bonnie, is everything okay? Did something happen?" Worry crept into Detective Patton's voice.

"Not really," she admitted. "A delivery guy came a day early, and it gave me a scare."

"I could see how that could make you think of this, Bonnie," the detective agreed. "But Bonnie, there's nothing. They're busy dealing with bigger problems right now. I covered your tracks. You're safe."

Bonnie felt anything but safe.

"You're sure?" she asked.

"As sure as I can be," he told her. "Our undercover agents haven't heard a thing. But listen, Bonnie. You need to trust your gut. If you don't feel safe, then leave."

"Okay, Mike." She took a deep breath. "Thanks."

"Anytime, Bonnie. If you need anything, you let me know. I'm here for you."

"Thanks, Mike."

She hung up the phone and slid it into her pocket. Thunder rumbled overhead. It was late in the day for their daily afternoon shower. It was an evening shower tonight. It reminded her of her first night here. The storm clouds were dark and ominous above her. The air crackled with anticipation of rain and lightning.

She fiddled with the phone, trying to calm her nerves.

She'd grown complacent. She'd grown comfortable here. She was fairly sure she was out of *their* reach, but then, who really knew?

A black sedan pulled up to the garage. The windows were tinted, and she didn't recognize the plates. It slowed, did a slow circle around the garage and then sped went back toward the main entrance. She ducked inside her cabin, staying low to the ground and peeking out of the window on the door.

Her heart was in her mouth. She knew, logically, that it was probably just a lost foster parent. That happened a lot around here. She knew that there was a decent amount of security given that billionaires lived on and owned the ranch. Most likely, it was nothing. But what if it wasn't? What if they were looking for her.

Anxiety gripped her chest and made it hard to breathe. Her heart wouldn't slow down, and she kept thinking she heard the sound of footsteps outside her cabin.

She couldn't stay here.

She needed to run. It was better if she ran now. It was better that she left before Tyson or Dylan became attached. If she left now, they would be disappointed, but they would forget her. If she left now, she could keep them safe.

Chapter 18

ylan

DYLAN WATCHED as big fat raindrops fell from dark skies. Rain splattered on the windshield of his truck in messy splotches as the storm rolled in. Lightning flashed in the distance, followed by a rolling boom of thunder.

The evening thunderstorm reminded him of the night Bonnie had arrived. The clouds were the same color, and the timing was similar. It made him smile. If the first storm had brought her into his life, he wondered what a second storm would bring.

He thought about their kiss last night. He worried that she was afraid of her ex coming back into the picture, but the way she'd spoken of him the other night made him think she was over the guy. She didn't talk about him. The ex seemed to be a thing of the past.

He pressed harder on the gas pedal of the truck. He wanted to get home to see her. He'd spent the day helping

Laura move a horse to a vet in Fort Collins. It had taken all day. He was glad the horse was doing well, but he hated that he'd missed the evening with Tyson and Bonnie. Spending time with the two of them was the highlight of his day.

He pulled the truck into the garage. He stood in the open garage door, looking out at the rain falling. It was mesmerizing to watch the big, fat drops plop onto the dry dirt and shake the needles on the pine tree. The smell was amazing. Fresh rain, dirt, and pine filled the air.

He wanted to see her. He thought about walking to her cabin. He knew a patch of wildflowers on the way. He thought of picking them to give her a bouquet. She deserved more. He thought of ordering flowers and having them delivered, but that didn't feel as personal as picking them himself. He wanted to do something nice to surprise her.

The temperature was dropping. Summer was swift in the mountains. The evenings stayed cool, and the rain always made it cold. It would only be a month or two before the frost came with these showers and they turned to snow.

He looked out to see Bonnie walking through the rain toward her car. She had her red duffle-bag slung over her shoulder as she bent against the rain. There was only one reason for her to be out in the rain with that bag.

She was leaving. His chest contracted hard against his heart. He didn't know why, but she was leaving.

He didn't pause. He just ran out into the rain. It was cold enough to take his breath away as he ran across the rough grass and the gravel paths. He sprinted through the rain, thunder rumbling around him as he splashed through puddles and mud.

"Bonnie!"

She tossed her bag into her trunk and turned to face him. Her hair was dark with rain.

"I can't stay, Dylan." She shook her head, her brow drawn and sad. "I'm so sorry."

"What?" He didn't understand. "Why?"

He stood there in the pouring rain, thunder all around them, his shirt turning from light blue to navy with rain and his feet in the mud. What had changed? All thoughts of flowers left his mind.

"Why?" he repeated. His chest ached.

She swallowed hard. "I'm not safe here. I can't stay."

He took a step forward. "You were going to leave without saying goodbye."

She shifted her weight and looked down at the ground. "I left a note in my room," she said softly. She looked up, the rain streaking her beautiful face. "I have to leave."

He took another step to her. His breath misted in the cold rain. She looked up at him, and he couldn't tell if it was rain or tears on her cheeks.

"What about Tyson?" he asked, keeping his voice quiet and calm.

She looked away from him. "He's better off without me."

"That's not true." He thought of how much she'd gotten the little orphan boy to open up in just over a week. Tyson needed her. He needed her.

"You're all better off without me," she whispered. She looked at him again, her brown eyes big and full of fear.

He reached out and brushed a strand of wet hair from her cheek. "That's certainly not true."

"You don't know," she told him, pulling away.

"Then tell me." He held his ground, the mist of his breath in the cold rain. The sound of thunder echoed between them.

She held still for a moment as if debating herself. Her

eyes focused on him and her chin rose. "I'm not running from an ex-boyfriend. I'm running from the mob."

He wasn't expecting that. He blinked twice. "What?" Bonnie visibly sighed. She looked simultaneously like she had already told this story a million times and like she desperately wanted someone to confide in. "Please, at least come inside with me and tell me before you go."

Her eyes lowered, then turned back toward her car. "You did fix my car. I guess I owe you that much."

Dylan shook his head. "You don't owe me anything, but I'd like to think that you can at least trust me enough to hear the real story before you go."

Her shoulders slumped. "Okay. But it's kind of a long one, so let's go inside."

He smiled, then put his arm around her as they walked inside.

Chapter 19

onnie

As soon as they were back inside, she threw her bag by the door and sat on the bed. Bonnie sighed. *Better clear up the little white lies I told first*, she thought.

"There really was a fire, but it wasn't started by an ex-boyfriend."

Dylan nodded at the confession, but didn't seem fazed by the fact that she had told a little white lie.

"When I got there, I knew it was a message. And the message wasn't for me, it was for my little brother," she said.

"Your brother? The security guard?"

Bonnie nodded. "He witnessed a murder. Unfortunately, the murder was a professional hit by a crime family called the Trio. They're a small organized crime group, but they're growing. He's in Witness Protection now."

Dylan frowned. "So what led you to here?"

Bonnie sighed again, then began to tell the story.

SHE TOLD Dylan everything that happened in her dream. The fire. The man in the crowd. The gesture he made. The overwhelming feeling of dread that she felt.

She looked around, trying to figure out where the man with the scar could have gone. There was a large crowd of people, but he wasn't with them. She searched the crowd. They were all watching her townhouse burn. No other houses were on fire yet, and she hoped they wouldn't catch. At least her brother wasn't here. He was safe somewhere with the police watching him.

"Are you okay, Bonnie?"

She nearly threw a punch at the person touching her shoulder. Luckily, Detective Patton ducked and pulled away before she had the chance to hit him. She felt bad about nearly clocking her neighbor. He was probably upset that his townhouse was nearly on fire too.

"Sorry, Mike." She pulled her arm into her chest. "I'm just spooked. Did you see the guy over there?"

Detective Mike Patton followed her gaze to the edge of the parking lot. "Who exactly are you looking for? There's plenty of people over there. I see Mrs. Gonzales, Frank, Joe..."

"No, he has this scar on his cheek." She drew her finger just along her cheekbone. "I swear I saw him at my house the night Brett reported the murder. He gave me the creeps."

Patton's face darkened. "Are you sure?"

She nodded. "The scar is pretty distinctive."

"Dark hair? And you said the scar was across his right cheek? Not the left?" Detective Patton asked, putting both his hands on her shoulders. "Are you sure?"

She nodded. "Yeah. Do you know who he is?"

Detective Patton swallowed hard. "He's the Trio's hitman. Are you sure you saw a scar?"

The Trio. They were the up-and-coming organized crime syndicate. They were the ones that Brett had witnessed and was going to testify against.

She hated that she had to nod. "Yeah."

"I want you to go stay next to the fire truck," he said, taking her arm and guiding toward the large red vehicle. Police officers and firefighters were everywhere. "Do you have your bags packed in the car like I told you to?"

"Of course. I put everything in there the first night just like you said."

"Good." He paused and looked her in the eye. She'd known him as her neighbor for the past two years, but she'd never seen this expression on his face. His face was stoic and stern, but she could see a flicker of fear in the back of his eyes. He was worried about her.

"What's going on, Mike?" Her voice came out as a whisper.

"If I'm right, you're going to need to get out of town for a while," he said quietly. He looked over at the fire. "God, I hope I'm wrong."

***

"He wasn't wrong, was he?" Dylan asked.

Bonnie shook her head. "It gets worse, though."

***

She remembered the fire chief saying that the cause of the fire was her stove. He said that she'd placed a book too close to the gas cook-top and it had caught fire. She said that was impossible, but the fire investigator was adamant. She had put the book there.

According to his report, she'd set the paperback copy of a book called, "You're Next" on the stove. It was a crime thriller by an author she'd never even heard of. She had told the police it wasn't her book, but there was no way to prove it.

The investigator made sure the cops said the fire was an accident. It was his signature on the report that said this fire had nothing to do with the Trio. Since the police had no evidence of a threat against her, they couldn't protect her. They didn't have the manpower or money to protect her without proof that the Trio was after her to get to Brett.

She was on her own.

Except, Detective Patton believed her. He didn't believe that the fire was an accident for even a minute. He knew the fire was a warning to both her and her brother, even if he couldn't prove it. The Trio crime organization didn't want her brother to testify.

He was the one who told her to run. He helped her as much as he could.

She was just glad she'd already put her important belongings in her car the night of the murder. Detective Patton had told her to do it as a precaution. She was still packed the day of the fire, so she had enough clothes for a couple of weeks and all of her legal papers. She'd nearly left her photo albums in the house, but had tucked them in at the last minute. She knew she was lucky in that regard.

DYLAN SAT THERE FOR A MOMENT, then whistled. "Sounds like they need a new investigator."

Bonnie burst out laughing without meaning to. "Yeah, he's a real piece of work."

"Your brother's dead set on testifying, then?"

Bonnie nodded. "He has always done the right thing, and there's no guarantee the Trio would leave us alone even if he decided to back down now. But they're still going to try.

And the police apparently don't have the funds or enough evidence to prove I'm in danger, so I'm on my own. That's why I have to leave."

She stomped over to where she had kept her bag and slung it over her shoulder. Before Dylan had a chance to say anything, she was out the door again. She knew that he was going to try to get her to stay, and she knew she had to keep her resolve. For Dylan, and Tyson, and Mia, and all the residents of this ranch.

She didn't hear anyone coming, and she was so revved up that she screamed a little when he put his hand on her shoulder. The emotion of the moment was too much, and she buried her head in Dylan's chest as the rain came down all around them.

He wrapped his arms around her, and for a brief moment, she felt safe.

Chapter 20

Bonnie shook in the wind like a leaf. All he wanted to do was keep his arms wrapped around her and protect her. It was strange. He was actually relieved there wasn't an ex. There wasn't someone she was pining over. This was the one time the mob was actually the better option.

"You don't have to run," he told her. His arms ached to pull her to him. He took a step forward, and she retreated from him.

"I can't do this to you," she whispered. He barely heard it over the rain.

She looked up at him, her eyes big and soft. Her delicate features were wet with rain and her hair plastered to her head. It reminded him of the night they met. She was still the most beautiful thing he'd ever seen.

Thunder growled around them, and the wind shook the trees. But they were in their own world. Just the two of them.

He barely felt the rain. He wasn't cold anymore. He needed her to stay. He could feel it in his bones that she was the one.

He wiped a raindrop, or perhaps it was a tear, from her face. She closed her eyes at his touch and leaned into his hand.

"I thought you were beautiful the first time I saw you in the rain," he told her. She opened her eyes to look at him, her cheek still pressed into his palm. "Please don't leave."

"But the mob--"

"I have security," he interrupted. "Mia has a security team. Carter has a security team. Hell, Laura has a security team, and I'm pretty sure that Carter has another security system on top of all of that that I don't even know about."

He moved toward her so that their bodies touched. She was shivering.

"You're safe here," he told her, his hand still on her cheek. "You're wanted here."

Her bottom lip went between her teeth as her eyes searched his face. Her breath came a little faster against him. "I am?"

She wasn't talking about security. She was making sure that she was his.

"Very much," he assured her. He tipped his head, pressing his lips to hers. It was gentle, but she whimpered as she let him kiss her. Her body leaned into him, wanting more.

"Okay," she whispered, her words soft against his lips. "I'll stay."

His heart surged with joy. He kissed her again.

Chapter 21

"FOLLOW ME," Dylan whispered, his lips barely leaving hers. Bonnie nodded, and he took her hand.

She held Dylan's hand firmly as they traversed through the storm, making their way toward his trailer. She already felt better about everything. Partly because the weight was off of her shoulders. She had come forward with the truth about why she was running. Dylan had believed her, and he had promised that he would keep her safe. She believed he would.

"Just a little further." Dylan squeezed her hand and continued leading her across the field.

The rain was coming down in sheets, and there was virtually no visibility. She clung to him, trusting him to find his way to his home. They passed the camp cabins and went to the edge of the property.

"We're here," he announced.

Bonnie breathed a sigh of relief. She lifted her head, squinting against the rain.

"This is your cabin?" she asked.

"I asked Carter if I could use a trailer instead," Dylan explained, going and opening the door for her. "It's more private, and it feels more like home. There are some perks to being me."

She chuckled and looked in awe at his home. It looked more like a small house than it did a trailer, at least any trailer she had ever seen. It was twice the length of a Greyhound bus, except taller. It looked like there were two separate levels to it, with a railing around what she assumed was a rooftop deck.

Dylan held the door open as she stepped inside. The dry warmth of the inside felt amazing. She was shivering with the cold and was fairly sure she would never feel warm again. Every article of clothing she was wearing was drenched with the freezing rain.

"It feels good in here," she said, rubbing her hands over her arms.

"Let me turn up the heat a little bit, though," he said. "You must be freezing."

He took a few steps down the center aisle of the trailer and touched some buttons on the thermostat. Bonnie took the chance to look around, and she was amazed by what she saw.

At the far end of the trailer was the kitchen. It was complete with granite countertops and stainless steel appliances. It even had one of those small refrigerators made for the sole purpose of storing wine. From where she stood, it looked like it was completely stocked with bottles, too.

From the floor to the ceiling, everything inside was extravagant. It looked like the editor of Home and Garden magazine had an unlimited budget to decorate his home, covering everything with only the finest furnishings.

"Let me get you a towel so you can dry off a bit." Dylan disappeared down to the end of the trailer opposite the kitchen. Bonnie followed him a little ways, passing through a small door that led into a completely different area.

There was a huge television screen on one wall. Across from that, was a brown leather sectional couch. It looked so soft and cozy. It took a lot of willpower to keep Bonnie from running over to it and collapsing. The fact that she was soaking wet helped. She didn't want to ruin it.

In the center of the room was an expensive-looking oriental rug. She didn't know much about the world of rugs, but she knew when something was handmade. This particular rug, she knew, was most certainly not created by a machine.

She lost track of him as she looked around the room. He popped around the corner, holding a white t-shirt in one hand and a pair of silky-looking, black pajama bottoms in the other.

"Here, I have some dry clothes for you," he said, with a warm smile. "You'll get sick."

"I don't think that's how you get sick," Bonnie smirked playfully. "I'm pretty sure germs get you sick, not cold weather."

"Well, Doctor Bonnie," he replied, laughing. "You may be right. Still, though, you should put these on because you'll be much more comfortable."

She smiled and took the shirt and pants from him. "Yeah, I guess I can't argue with that. Is there somewhere that I can change?"

"Yes, of course." Dylan walked her through the door and to the very back room, which was obviously his grand suite.

The bedroom was by far the biggest area of the trailer that Bonnie had seen so far. It was furnished with a King-sized bed, which was covered in a thick white comforter. There were windows on all sides of the room, where she was able to see that the rain was still coming down outside.

The trailer was so large and spacious it felt like a house. She shuddered at the thought of having to drive it anywhere. But, then Dylan was wealthy enough to hire someone with a lot more experience to do that for him.

She followed Dylan the rest of the way into the room, where she noticed a beautiful painting hanging on one of the walls. It was a giant floor-to-ceiling mural of a cowboy on a horse. The colors were bold, and the image was roughly painted with broad strokes. It gave it a modern feel and added to the beauty of the room.

"I like the painting," she said.

"Do you?" he asked. "A friend of mine back home is an artist. He paints things like that all the time, but this particular one caught my eye. When I told him I wanted to buy it, he said it wasn't for sale. Instead, he ended up giving it to me for Christmas one year."

"That's a great friend," Bonnie said. "The picture is fitting for you."

"How do you mean?" Dylan frowned slightly as he looked up at the painting.

She shrugged. "There's a cowboy on a horse. You're living on a ranch now. It kind of makes a lot of sense."

Dylan nodded in agreement. "I actually didn't even think about that, but you're right. I liked this picture before I moved here, though. Long before I wanted to pretend to be a ranch hand." He flashed a flirtatious wink, then chuckled.

"The bathroom is right through that door," Dylan told her. "Go change and get dry. I'll change in here."

"Great," she said, trying to keep her teeth from chattering as a shiver trickled through her. She was still soaked to the bone, and even though the trailer was warm, she still had the chills. "I'll be out in a minute."

"Take your time," he said. "I set the dryer out onto the counter for you, in case you want to dry your hair. There's also a brush. That's about the extent of the girl-type things that I have here in the trailer."

Bonnie laughed. "That's plenty. Thanks, Dylan."

"No worries. There's also a clean towel in there for you," he replied, turning to leave. "Anyway, I'll go put on some hot water, and I'll have tea ready for you when you come out."

She just smiled and watched as he left the room. She held his clothes tightly to her chest and let out a long, relaxing breath.

He puts me at ease, she thought. *I don't know exactly what it is about him. I can't put my finger on it. There's just something about being around him that takes my worries away.*

Bonnie hadn't fully realized it until that moment, but since she had walked into the trailer with Dylan, she hadn't thought about her old life at all. Not once. Sure, it had only been about five minutes so far, but that was longer than she had gone in some time without worrying about the mob and what they would do to her if they ever found her.

Spending time with Dylan is like going on vacation, she thought, chuckling to herself as she went into the bathroom. *He's just another reason why I'm really starting to love it here at the ranch. I hope I get to spend more time with him. There's so much about him that I want to learn.*

"Oh my gosh," she whispered, stepping across the gray tile of the bathroom. She was expecting something simple given that this was a trailer, but that wasn't the case with this bathroom.

It was bigger and nicer than any trailer bathroom she could have imagined could fit in a space this size. To the right was the bathroom counter. It was made of beautiful white granite and ran the entire length of the wall. It had two sinks, one next to the other.

Above the counter was a mirror that covered the entire upper half of the wall. It was lit up on all sides by tiny blue LED lights. It gave the bathroom a comfortable glow. It was enough light to illuminate the entire space and allow her to see the over-sized shower at the back of the room. It was one of those showers that had more than one shower head. There were three upper ones and even a couple on the sides. In addition to that, there was a bench in there, so one could sit down and relax in the hot water and steam

She took a few more steps inside. The smell of Dylan's cologne entered her nose as she neared the counter. The scent was fresh like he had just sprayed it on a moment before. She took in a deep breath and smiled.

Standing in front of the mirror, Bonnie removed her wet clothes and set them on the counter between the sinks. Both her bra and panties were also soaked, and she knew that they would take forever to dry if she just put his clothes on top of them. So she took those off, too, setting them onto the counter next to the others.

Is it bad that I've only been in his trailer for just a few minutes and I'm already naked? She asked herself, with a quiet laugh.

Bonnie grabbed the towel from the counter and wrapped it around her body. Then she started up the hair dryer that Dylan had laid out for her. The heat from the dryer felt amazing and helped to warm her up a little bit.

She quickly brushed her hair as soon as it was dry and then got dressed in Dylan's clothes. Both the t-shirt and the pajama pants he had given her to wear were a bit baggy on her. That was to be expected, though, and she didn't really care. The clothes were dry and warm, and that was enough. Plus, there was something about wearing his clothes that made her smile. It almost made her feel like she was his girlfriend. She liked the idea.

When she stepped back into the bedroom, she heard some soft piano music coming from the opposite end of the trailer. She headed out and into the hallway. She passed through the living room again and was heading toward the kitchen when she noticed that the music was coming from above her.

A small, circular staircase was to her right. It was made of wrought iron and spiraled up to the second floor of the trailer.

"Dylan?" she called out but didn't get a response.

She continued to ascend the stairs to the top floor. When she got there, she glanced to her right, toward where the music was playing.

Seriously, though, a trailer with a second floor? She thought. *This place is bigger than my childhood home. Unbelievable.*

"Hey, Dylan, are you back here?" Bonnie walked softly down the carpeted hall until she got to the doorway. She poked her head in and saw that it was another bedroom, this one a bit smaller than the one downstairs. It was definitely where the music was coming from, though.

She took just one step inside, and when she glanced over, she saw Dylan standing at the foot of the bed. He had his back to her. The only thing he had on was a pair of gray sweatpants. His upper half was completely bare. She glanced away, but just for a split second. Then she couldn't help but look at him once again.

Bonnie knew that she'd just walked in on him while he

was changing out of his wet clothes. She was pretty certain that he didn't know she was there, though. The proper side of her realized that she should just turn around and head back downstairs. However, a different part of her wanted only to stand and stare. He was just too gorgeous not to.

The muscles in his shoulders and back flexed as he reached down to pick up a shirt from the top of a nearby chair. His tan skin was smooth and flawless. She wanted to run her fingers across his shoulders. Just looking at him caused her core to heat.

She knew she shouldn't stare. So, she forced herself to take a step back. But, because she wasn't watching where she was going, though, she backed right into the railing. It was just hard enough to make a thud. Her eyes widened, and her heart nearly leaped out of her mouth.

Dylan slowly turned around to the sound. He had just pulled his shirt over his head, but it was only halfway on. Bonnie could now see his ripped abdominal muscles. She probably would have enjoyed admiring the new view, except now she was far too embarrassed to enjoy much of anything.

"Oh, hey, Bonnie," Dylan said, pulling his shirt down the rest of the way. "Sorry, I didn't know you were there."

"Just walked up," she said.

She figured it was probably best to not mention the fact that she'd been standing there and staring at him for the past few minutes.

Dylan seemed pretty much unfazed by her presence, though. In fact, he had a little smirk on his face. It made Bonnie wonder if he had actually *had* known that she'd been standing there the whole time and that he hadn't done anything to stop it.

"I've got some tea brewing," he said. "I hope you like green jasmine."

"I love it," she said, glancing away a bit. Her cheeks tingled, and she was pretty certain she was blushing.

"Great." Dylan walked toward her. "Are you hungry? I'm sure I've got some things in the fridge."

"No, just tea would be good." Bonnie followed Dylan back downstairs and into the kitchen.

He approached the stove and grabbed the tea kettle, along with two blue teacups. Then he headed around the corner to where the dining room was. This room was noticeably smaller than the others, but still just as well designed. In the center was a quaint round table, with four chairs around it. Both the table and the chairs were made of thick, see-through plastic. It gave the room a very modern and clean feel.

Bonnie took a seat, and Dylan sat down in the chair across the table from her. He filled both cups with tea. They sipped their drinks quietly for a moment. Bonnie listened to the rain, just enjoying the sound and also the fact that she didn't have to be out in it anymore.

"It feels good to be dry," she said, setting her cup down.

"No kidding," he said. "I can't believe how hard it rained out there. That was intense."

Dylan gazed into Bonnie's eyes as he spoke, causing her to melt right there in the seat. His stare was intense but comforting. It made her feel safe and protected. She couldn't get over how much he made her feel that way. It was unlike anything she'd experienced with anybody else and that included witness protection.

"Thanks for the tea." Bonnie took another sip, letting the liquid warm her up from the inside. "It's really good."

"You're welcome," Dylan said, with a warm smile that

made Bonnie tingle all over once again. She loved the way he looked at her. She wanted to kiss him again. She wanted to feel the connection between the two of them again. She just needed to find a way to get there.

Bonnie ran her finger around the rim of the empty cup. It was just a habit, something that she did whenever she was deep in thought. She wasn't sure when she had picked it up, but it was definitely something she had done for years.

"Do you think I could maybe borrow these clothes for a night?" she asked. "I can wash them and get them back to you tomorrow. I just really don't want to put my wet clothes back on before I go home."

"Yes, of course," he said. "I have a ton of clothes here and I kind of think that outfit looks better on you than me. Why don't you just keep it?"

She ran her hands down her sides. "Really? It's so big on me."

Dylan shrugged. "I think it looks cute on you." His eyes were warm on her, and she loved the way he looked at her.

A few strands of her hair fell across her face, and she pushed them back over her ear. "Thank you."

She wasn't sure what to do. Part of her felt like she should stand up from the table and tell Dylan how much she appreciated the hospitality, before heading back home. It would have been the proper thing to do. The only problem was that she really didn't want to leave. She wanted to kiss him.

"Let's go to the living room. There's a big comfy couch in there that we can relax on for a bit," Dylan said, noticing her empty teacup. "Let's let the rainstorm pass at least before you head out."

"That sounds good." Bonnie stood up from her chair

and took a step back, allowing Dylan to pass by. He smiled at her as he did, and their eyes locked for just a moment.

That look of his, she thought. *There's just something in his eyes that I love so much. It just makes me trust him. Am I crazy, though? Am I crazy to allow myself to start falling for a guy here at the ranch? I mean I don't even know how long I'll be here. What if I go home sooner rather than later? What if he breaks my heart? What if, what if, what if...*

Bonnie's mind whirled, but it didn't stop her body from following Dylan to the living room.

When they got there, he took a seat on the couch. Bonnie sat next to him, taking the opportunity to get close. The cushions pulled her in, and she let out a long, relaxed breath.

"This feels nice," she said, turning to look at Dylan.

He seemed just as relaxed. He had one arm over the back of the couch and had already kicked his feet up onto the coffee table.

The two of them sat close. Dylan became like a magnet to her body. She just wanted to touch him and to lose herself in him in a way that she didn't quite understand. She snuggled into his shoulder with his arm draped over her. He was so warm. She felt like purring.

"It's a good thing you decided to stay," Dylan said, pointing toward the window across from them. "Looks like the storm is just getting started."

"Oh, wow." Bonnie's jaw dropped as she looked out the window.

Dylan wasn't kidding. The storm that was brewing in the distance looked much worse than the one they'd just walked through. The clouds were so dark that virtually no sun was passing through them. Even though it was early afternoon, it started to look like late evening outside.

The storm moved quickly, too. She watched as the storm crossed the sky in just a matter of moments. The rain came once again, though this time it was somehow more intense than the first.

"This is insane," she said, turning to face him.

The only light in the room was that which came from the window, and since the sun was covered up, that didn't really amount to much. Still, it was enough to illuminate Dylan's gorgeous face. His dark hair was pushed over to the side, and there was stubble on his cheeks.

They gazed at each other for just a moment. Then Bonnie heard an electric-sounding crackle outside. Before she could even turn to look, a lightning bolt hit a nearby tree. It sent a shock wave of energy toward them, and she screamed in surprise.

Without even thinking about it, she jumped toward Dylan, wrapping her arms around the back of his neck. Within a split second, she had brought her knees toward her chest and managed to get herself into a position where she was now curled up in his lap. Her eyes were wide with fright when she glanced up to Dylan.

"Wow," she said, her hands trembling. "That was close."

Dylan wrapped his arm around her, holding her against him. She could feel her own heart beating quickly in her chest. She didn't know if the adrenaline that was pumping through her veins was caused by the nearby lightning strike or by the fact that she was now sitting on Dylan's lap.

"Sorry," she said. "That scared me."

"Don't be sorry," he replied. "I'll be honest. It made me jump a little bit, too. That was about as close as it gets. I'm pretty sure it hit the tree right outside of the trailer."

Attraction crackled in the air between them. It was more powerful than the lightning outside.

She knew what she wanted right then. It wasn't just to kiss Dylan. She wanted to lower her walls down for someone. For the first time since her brother got in trouble, Bonnie felt like she had someone she could turn to. That alone caused the magnetic pull to increase in intensity.

"Kiss me," she said, but her words were so quiet that she didn't know if any actual sound came out at all. It didn't matter, though. Even if she'd only said it in her mind, Dylan still got the hint.

They leaned toward each other, gently pressing their lips together. The simple kiss took Bonnie's breath away and caused goose bumps to pop up on her skin.

For a moment, time stopped. As she sat on Dylan's lap, with her lips pressed to his, all of her cares flew out the window. It was just her and Dylan and the rain outside. Nothing else existed.

Without pulling her lips away, Bonnie situated herself so that she was straddling over Dylan's lap. She closed her eyes, letting touch be her only sense. She brought one of her hands up and placed it on his cheek. His beard stubble tickled her fingertips as she gently slid her hand down toward his neck. The smell of his cologne made its way into her nose. It was intoxicating, and she breathed it in, allowing the scent to turn her on.

She felt Dylan's hands as he placed them on her sides, just above her hips. He held her by her sides, with his strong but comforting grip. She felt safe with him.

Bonnie gently broke the kiss. She could see her own reflection in his eyes. They were both breathing a little harder now. Her lips tingled from the kiss.

Neither of them said a word. They just sat there, gazing at each other as though they were long lost lovers that were finally reunited. To Bonnie, it almost felt like she had known

Dylan in a different life. It was as though she was meant to come to that farm and meet him. He was where she was supposed to be.

Bonnie's hands drifted up his arms, where she savored the feeling of his muscles as they flexed underneath her fingertips. She let herself focus on the feeling. There was no need to rush. She didn't see the hurry or the need to force anything to happen that didn't unfold naturally.

She tilted her head, then parted her lips to allow his tongue in a bit further. A soft moan found its way out of her throat but was muffled by their kiss.

Dylan's breathing became heavier. She could feel his chest rising and falling against her own quick breaths. She could sense his passion and the lust behind his kiss.

He placed his hand on her cheek and then gently cradled her chin between his thumb and forefinger. His touch sent a pleasurable chill through Bonnie, causing her to open her eyes.

"You're so beautiful," he whispered.

She'd heard those words before, but never fully believed them. Dylan was genuine. He said it as though he were stating a simple fact like gravity pulls or the sky is blue. He really believed that Bonnie *was* beautiful.

It was more than just his words that told her that, though. It was the way he held her like she was precious to him. It was also in his eyes. It was in the way he was looking at her right then. That look said more to her than words ever could.

Dylan dropped his hand back down to her thighs. Then he slowly stood up from the couch, lifting Bonnie up as he did. She wrapped her legs around his waist, keeping her arms draped over his shoulders. She didn't ask where he was taking her because she didn't care. As long as she was with him, she wouldn't have even minded if he'd taken her outside into the middle of the storm.

She leaned in and kissed his neck, breathing in the scent of his cologne once more. She loved the way it smelled. It was masculine and potent. She couldn't get enough.

Dylan carried her with ease across the living room. His muscular arms cradled her against his body as he made his way through the back door and into the master suite. Anticipation flowed through her.

He carried her to the bedroom and gently laid her on the bed. She relaxed her arms above her head as she sunk into the down comforter. Dylan crawled over the top of her and leaned in. This time, he didn't bring his lips to hers. Instead, he went right past them and kissed the outside of her neck, just below her ear.

She closed her eyes halfway, overwhelmed by desire. Dylan continued kissing her neck, inching his lips downward toward the top of her shoulder. Meanwhile, her hands drifted up and down his muscular arms, almost as if they had a mind of their own. Her legs were still wrapped around his waist, too, and she was using them to pull Dylan closer to her.

He moved slowly and sensually. There was no aggression in the way he touched her. It was gentle and calm. He moved as though there was no place in the world he would rather be right then. He made Bonnie feel like the center of his attention, which in turn made her feel sexier than she had felt in some time.

She noticed that his breathing had become even heavier and there was a look of lust written across his face. His eyes had dilated a bit, and he clenched his jaw as he gazed at her. He wanted her as much as she wanted him.

"Come here," she said, placing a hand on his cheek and urging him to lean toward her.

He didn't hesitate to do as she asked. He leaned in, and two of them kissed again. This time, their tongues collided immediately, twisting into a sensual dance.

The intensity between them increased with each passing second. She began to ache with anticipation and raw desire. She wanted to see and feel more of Dylan. She wanted him to sooth the desperation that now filled her.

She broke the kiss and immediately realized that she was panting now. Her breaths were quick, mimicking the throbbing between her thighs. She wanted this. Even if she couldn't keep it forever, she wanted this now.

"Never leave, Bonnie," he whispered, his voice raw.

Bonnie parted her lips to respond, but before she could, Dylan leaned in and kissed her once more. She closed her eyes and enjoyed his touch. Any walls that she had had up, or any hesitations she'd been harboring, were now gone. She was ready and willing to give herself to him in every way.

She dropped her hands down Dylan's sides, gripping the bottom of his t-shirt. She pulled it up to his chest, then began feeling his bare stomach. The sensation of his muscular abdominal muscles underneath her fingers turned her on. It was like touching a washboard. Every muscle was defined and toned.

Dylan broke the kiss and sat back on his heels to finished pulling his shirt off. Bonnie watched intently as he exposed his upper half. He tossed his shirt carelessly to the floor beside the bed and smiled. Her whole body trembled at his gaze.

Dylan dropped down and began kissing Bonnie's neck again. This time, her hands went to his back. She felt his flesh as she dragged her fingers downward along his shoulders and to his spine.

He kissed downward toward her shoulder. Bonnie wanted him to go further, though. She wanted him to kiss her all over and was done wearing these over-sized clothes anyway.

"Take my shirt off," she said.

It was supposed to come out sounding like a suggestion but ended up coming out more like a demand. Dylan sat up again and carefully peeled her t-shirt upward, exposing her belly. She bit her bottom lip as she watched him as if to subliminally tell him to keep going.

He didn't stop there. He continued pushing up her shirt until it slid over her breasts, exposing them to the air.

"God, you're gorgeous," he whispered, as he looked Bonnie up and down. An aching hunger flashed in his eyes. She knew her own mirrored his.

Dylan had her shirt bunched up at the top of her chest. She finished what he had started, grabbing the t-shirt and quickly pulling it over her head. She tossed it to the side.

Now they were both topless. The kisses were better now that there was no cloth between them. Their flesh was pressed against each other. Her chest was touching his, and she could feel her nipples growing firm.

Dylan felt it too, his hands holding on harder. She could feel him harden against her, pressing against her hips. She wanted more. She wanted all of him.

"Yes," she whispered, breaking the kiss. "Take me, Dylan."

The words just tumbled out of her mouth without much thought. It was almost as though the filter part of her brain had taken a vacation and the only part of it that was still working was the instinctual, carnal part.

Dylan brought his lips to the front of her neck. He kissed each inch as he moved his face downward, between her cleavage. She glanced down, watching as he moved a bit to the right. Without any hesitation, he wrapped his lips around her nipple, sending another burst of pleasure into her.

He let out a soft growl and then began to quickly move his tongue up and down, flicking it against her sensitive nipple. Waves of sensation washed over her, causing her jaw to clench and her back to arch. It felt so good being touched by him. If she had any cares left in her mind at that point, they were now long gone, washed down the gutters along with the rain.

Dylan slowly pulled back. Her nipple popped out of his mouth, making a wet kissing sound as it did. He immediately moved his face over, giving equal pleasure to her other breast.

She was breathing harder than before, her chest pressing into Dylan's face with each inhale. The aching desire between her legs had no become a throbbing desperation. She wanted to have him inside of her so badly. Her body begged for it.

Without even realizing what she was doing, she gently pressed onto the top of Dylan's head, urging him to move his face down along her body. He didn't resist at all. He pulled away from her other nipple, then brought his lips to the center of her chest. He then went straight down, kissing a line toward her belly button. When he got there, he glanced up at Bonnie with dark eyes of desire.

His pupils were dilated, and the expression on his face told her how turned on he was. It seemed like he was ready to rip her pants off right there. Which she would have been fine with.

They locked eyes for just a moment, then Dylan continued kissing downward. He stopped when he got to the elastic waist strap of her pajama pants and looked up. He waited for her nod to continue.

Dylan pulled downward on the elastic strap, taking everything off. He peeled the clothing until it was wrapped around her knees. He gazed at her naked body and shook his head in awe. He didn't say anything, though. He just admired her. She felt beautiful under his gaze.

He lifted her legs up and slipped her clothing off, tossing it to the side with their shirts.

He kissed the inside of her ankle, then slid his lips a little ways up her calf. He turned his head, bringing his mouth to her other leg. Back and forth he switched off, kissing the inner part of her leg and moving upwards with each movement. He passed her knees, then a moment later, was midway up the inside of her thighs.

She could hear her heart beating now. It made a whooshing sound, as blood pumped past her eardrums. She was so turned on already that it felt like she could explode.

Dylan took his time, kissing her legs all the way. He moved carefully, as though he was afraid he'd miss touching a single spot. She loved it, though. She loved the way he seemed to cherish her.

By the time he got to the upper part of her thigh, she was squirming on the bed. All she wanted was for him to kiss her most sensitive area.

"You're killing me," she said, with a groan. Her back arched, barely able to breathe with the sheer weight of desire pressing down on her.

He glanced up at her and smirked, then immediately dropped his face down between her legs. He gave her exactly what she wanted.

Dylan darted his tongue out and tasted her. A burst of pleasure shuttered through her body. She leaned her head back, gripping the blanket beneath her. She closed her eyes, reveling in the pleasure he gave.

He started slow, his hands holding her thighs as he sent wave after wave of pleasure directly into her core. He moved his tongue and teeth, finding new ways to make her cry out in ecstasy with every lick, suck, and nibble.

Her eyes rolled up to the heavens, and her back continued to arch. She reveled in the sensations, letting her body relax into him and accept the pleasure he offered.

He brought her to the tipping point. Her mind lost its hold on reality as she fell over into dizzy sweetness. Delicious oblivion swallowed her, and she cried out his name.

Dylan pleasured her for a little longer, then finally pulled his face away. When Bonnie opened her eyes, she saw him crawl off the bed. He stood on the floor and slipped his thumbs into the waist of his own sweatpants.

"Please, Dylan," she groaned, releasing her grip from the blankets. Her release was not enough to satiate the hunger deep within her. She needed him. She needed him inside of her, filling her and joining them together.

"I like the way you say my name." Dylan slipped off his pants and kicked them to the side.

Dylan grabbed a condom from the nightstand. In less than two breaths, he was back with her, pressed at her entrance. Around them, the air charged. There was a soft vibration running through her skin, calling him to her. She raised her hips, asking him without words to take her.

"Please, Dylan," she whispered again. His dark eyes ignited with desire. Hunger and need filled his face as he pressed forward. She gasped as he filled her. Her jaw dropped, and her eyes rolled into the back of her head. The desperate throbbing between her legs had ceased and was replaced with an overwhelming pleasure.

He rocked into her, groaning with the pleasure of it. Dylan placed his hands onto the bed, just above Bonnie's shoulders. The soft light caressed the flexed muscles of his shoulders and biceps, accenting his strength around her.

She reached around to his back, gently digging her fingernails into his skin. She kissed him, needing as many connections as their body could make. The passion in the room was intoxication. It wasn't just lust, though. There was more to it than that. Bonnie could sense that this was different than just simple sex. It was more potent, more real.

The pleasure that she experienced wasn't just in her body. It was in her emotions, too. All of her senses filled with bliss. Her walls were down, and she thought that was making her able to connect on other levels with Dylan besides just the physical.

He wrapped his arms around her and rolled. She slid away from him, keenly feeling the loss. He now lay on his back before her, so she scrambled to resume her place with him, straddling her legs around his hips.

They both let out a groan of pleasure as Bonnie dropped her weight, allowing him inside once again. She felt complete this way.

Another bolt of lightning hit nearby. It sounded like it was just outside of the trailer again. However, this one didn't make Bonnie jump at all. In fact, she was so deep in her lust that she hardly even heard it. It sounded distant, the way people sounded when she'd hold her breath and go underwater at a swimming pool. It seemed like the storm outside was far away.

Now that she was on top, she controlled the pace. She rode him slowly at first, rocking her body back and forth.

The ache inside of her grew, and she quickened her pace. His hands went to her breasts, cupping and fondling them as they bounced. She loved the roughness of his fingertips against the sensitive skin of her delicate flesh. She loved the way he panted, his chest rising and falling, not with exertion, but sheer desire.

She was losing control, and he was coming along with her. Her legs tightened, and she called out his name.

They came together. Or at least, she thought they did. She wasn't totally sure because everything was lost to pleasure and the sensation of him losing himself within her. Together they were both lost and found at the same time.

After a few moments, Dylan finally took a ragged breath and opened his eyes. He shook his head in awe as he gazed at Bonnie. Then he took her hands, gently pulling her into his embrace.

They kissed again. This time, it was slow and sensual. They had expelled much of their energy, and all that was left was sweet, sexy little pecks on the lips.

She didn't want to be apart from him. Not ever. She wanted to stay there for eternity with him, just kissing and making love, pretending that the rest of the world didn't exist. Pretending that everything was fine. Making believe that the mob wasn't after her and that there wasn't an ever-present danger everywhere else in the world besides the ranch and in that trailer with Dylan.

The rain outside had slowed down. The only thing left was the sound of a drizzle as it hit the ground. Bonnie gently parted her kiss and laid her head on Dylan's chest. While she listened to his heartbeat, she gazed out the nearby window. The sun looked like it was about to peek from behind the clouds. She almost wished that it wouldn't, though. She wanted to remain safe inside the storm with him.

Dylan wrapped his arm around her shoulder, holding her close. Her breathing slowed, the effects of the rain and sex finally catching up to her. With his arms protecting her, she finally could relax. For the first time in weeks, she slept without fear of nightmares.

Chapter 22

onnie

"THIS TIME, we're going to go underwater," Bonnie told Tyson. "You can totally do this."

Tyson looked unconvinced. "Can we wait for Dylan?"

"Sure," she replied with a shrug. "Or you can show him a new trick when he gets here."

Tyson thought about it, and Bonnie let him have his time to think. She loved these lessons with Tyson. The kid was turning into a regular fish. He still didn't like the sensation of water on his ears, but he was getting used to it. The more they worked together, the more progress Tyson made. She was so proud of him. She knew it wasn't easy for the kid.

Dylan usually joined them for lessons, but today he was running late. She was looking forward to having him join them more than Tyson was.

"Okay," Tyson announced. He took a deep breath and dunked his head underwater for approximately half a second. It wasn't much, but he came up looking both terrified and incredibly pleased with himself.

"That was amazing!" Bonnie praised. The terrified look slowly faded from Tyson's eyes. "Dylan is going to be super impressed. I know I am."

"There he is," Tyson said, waving to a figure across the pool.

Bonnie turned to look, and her heart skipped a beat. She loved that it did that. Dylan waved back to the two of them as he set his things on the edge of the pool and stripped down to his swim trunks. She had a feeling it would never get old to watch him take his clothes off.

"Hi, Dylan," she called. A smile filled her face, and her heart did happy somersaults when she saw him. He waved and continued to set his things down on the edge of the pool.

"Are you two gonna get married?" Tyson asked.

"What?" Bonnie sputtered and did a double take as she turned to the boy.

"Are you gonna marry Dylan?" Tyson repeated.

"Why would you ask that?" Bonnie could feel the blush heating her face.

"Because you have a funny smile on your face when you look at him. He gets the same one when he looks at you," Tyson explained. "I noticed since you had me practice looking at faces."

Bonnie chuckled. She'd been helping Tyson practice emotions by looking at faces and tell her what they were feeling. It was something she did with her autism students, and it seemed to help Tyson figure out his own emotions as well.

"You are doing a good job of looking at faces and recognizing emotions," she told him, patting his shoulder. She was having a hard time trying to come up with the appropriate way to explain this.

"So you are?" Tyson asked. His young face was so innocent. "I would like that."

"Well, he does make me happy," she told him. "But, marriage is a big step. I like him a lot, but I don't think we're ready yet. It's important not to rush into a marriage."

"Oh. Okay." Tyson shrugged and then went back to blowing bubbles in the pool as he waited for Dylan to get in the water.

Bonnie shook her head. If only she had the innocence of a five-year-old. Life was so much simpler in his world. Love led to marriage and happily ever afters. The bad guys always lost. She wished the world was as black and white as Tyson viewed it. As safe.

From the corner of her eye, she saw a security guard make a round. Dylan and Carter had both increased the patrols. Since telling Dylan her situation, she had also told Mia.

She'd been afraid that Mia would fire her. Instead, Mia had shrugged and said she figured as much. Something about her background check had tipped her off that there was police interference in Bonnie's life. Mia had already had security increased the day she offered her the position. Bonnie had to wonder just what else Mia had been able to figure out about her.

"How's my swimmer?" Dylan asked, walking through the waist-high water to where Tyson happily blew bubbles.

"Watch this!" Tyson took a deep breath, and once again dunked himself in the water. He didn't go deep enough to completely submerge his hair, but it was definitely progress.

"Wow, buddy!" Dylan praised as Tyson came back up.

"That was so great. You must have worked really hard on that."

Tyson beamed at him. "I did. Bonnie helped me."

"Well, since you can do that, I think I have a new game for us to play," Dylan told him. He looked up at Bonnie, and she nodded.

"What kind of game?" Tyson asked, excited.

Dylan grinned. "It's called, 'Shark Attack.'" He snapped his teeth. "So, you better swim little fishies, because this shark is *hungry!*"

Tyson shrieked with delight and scrambled to get away as Dylan started to sing the traditional "Jaws" music as he moved through the water. Bonnie laughed, watching the two of them.

"You're not safe either, little fish," he told her. She raised her eyebrows at him, wondering just what he was going to do.

"Watch out, Bonnie! He's gonna eat you!" Tyson shouted from the shallow end.

"Damn straight," Dylan murmured, quiet enough that Tyson couldn't hear the curse word. He grinned and lunged for her.

Bonnie shrieked and dove to the side, but he was faster than she expected. His hand grazed her leg and wrapped around her ankle. She tried to kick free, but he had her. He proceeded to pull her under the water and dunk her.

She came up sputtering. She pushed her hair out of her eyes. "You are so shark fin soup, buddy."

Dylan chuckled as she lunged for him. He was fast and moved out of the way, but she was ready. She ducked under the water and pushed off the bottom of the pool to get speed. She caught him as he ran from her, wrapping her arms around his neck and clinging to his back like a monkey.

He laughed and tried to shake her off, but she held on. He dove under the water, trying to knock her off with speed, but she was ready and held on.

"Wee! Dolphin ride," she announced as he surfaced and stood. "Dunk!"

She threw her weight back into the pool, knocking him off balance. Together, they toppled backward into the water. She let go and swam away.

He came up sputtering this time, his dark hair falling in his face. He shook his head and grinned at her. She loved the way his dark eyes sparkled and danced as he looked at her. He motioned his head toward the shallow end, where Tyson was watching the two of them and laughing.

She nodded. It was time to get the little one.

"SHARK ATTACK!" Dylan yelled as they both rushed the shallow end. Tyson's eyes went big, and he scrambled to get away, but the two adults had him cornered.

Bonnie got him first. "Om nom nom," she growled, coming up and tickling his ribs with her fingers. Tyson shrieked with laughter, trying to wiggle away as Bonnie pretended to eat him up. He splashed and kicked until he freed himself, but Dylan was ready for him.

He picked up the boy and waded out into deeper water. Dylan put his hands under Tyson's arms and threw him into the air. Tyson flew up, and Dylan caught him with a splash just as the boy was to hit the water. Dylan didn't let the boy's head go under, but let enough of his body enter the water to make a great big splash.

"Again! Again!" Tyson shouted, his face so full of smile it looked like he was going to split apart at the seams with joy.

Dylan tossed him into the air again, his strong arms

flexing with the weight. Tyson screamed with delight as Bonnie moved out to join them in the deeper water.

"Catch Bonnie!" Dylan told her, throwing the boy over the water into her ready hands. She was ready to catch the small boy as he flew over the water to her.

Tyson laughed as a splash of water covered the two of them. "Tyson ball!" Bonnie yelled, using all her strength to toss him the two feet back to Dylan.

Dylan caught him with ease, and the three of them doubled over with laughter. Water, laughter, and smiles filled the air.

This is perfect, Bonnie thought, watching as Dylan made Tyson shriek with delight by throwing him up in the air and catching him as he hit the water. Her heart hurt she was so happy in this moment. She decided she could stay here forever. This was home now. They were home.

ylan

"Can I go eat with my friends tonight?" Tyson asked as they neared the cafeteria.

Dylan squeezed the boy's shoulder. Tyson was helping him with a surprise for Bonnie. "I think that would be fine."

"Um, sure," Bonnie agreed. She frowned slightly but shrugged. "Whatever makes you happy."

"Thanks." Tyson grinned at the two of them and then attempted a wink to Dylan.

"Get out of here," Dylan told him with a chuckle. He smiled as the boy ran to catch up with his two bunk-mates. He waved before disappearing inside the building.

"So are we doing something special then?" Bonnie asked, crossing her arms and raising her eyebrows at him.

"What makes you think that?" he replied, feigning innocence.

"Because that was just way too obvious," she told him.

"Tyson can't keep a secret to save his life. He already told me you have something planned."

"That little traitor." Dylan shook his head, but couldn't help but smile. Tyson was such a good kid. Dylan hadn't bonded with any of the kids here quite like he had with Tyson. He adored the little orphan, even if the kid couldn't keep a secret.

"So? What are we doing?" Bonnie asked, nudging his arm with her hand. "I'm hungry."

He turned and looked at her.

"You sure are beautiful, you know that?" he said.

She raised an eyebrow. "Dylan, my hair is a mess, and I'm not wearing any makeup at all. All of that, on top of the fact that I'm in a wet swimsuit and sweatpants. I hardly think I look beautiful right now."

She obviously doesn't know how I see her, he thought.

To Dylan, she looked incredible, despite the fact that she didn't have makeup on and her hair was a little out of place. He thought she looked just as good without makeup and it wasn't her hair that he was falling in love with. It was *her*. She could have been wearing ripped overalls and covered in tractor grease, and he would have felt the same way about her. It was something in her energy, something in her smile. He couldn't quite put his finger on it, but whatever it was had him head over heels for her. It was unlike anything he'd experienced in his life.

"Well, I still think you look really pretty anyway," Dylan said.

Bonnie's cheeks turned a light shade of red as she blushed. It made Dylan smile seeing her flush at the complement. Without saying another word, he leaned in and gave her a quick kiss on the cheek. When he pulled away, Bonnie's eyes were lit up in her face was beaming with happiness.

"You're really sweet. You know that?" She said.

Dylan shrugged. "I'm just being honest."

"I like that." Bonnie innocently shuffled her feet in the dirt.

"How do you feel about dinner at my place?" Dylan asked, raising an eyebrow.

Bonnie brought her gaze up to meet his. "Is that the surprise?"

"You don't sound too excited," Dylan said.

"It's not that," Bonnie said. "I just didn't know you cooked."

Dylan laughed. "I don't cook. I have tried, but I am extremely unsuccessful at it. Chef's making chicken cacciatore tonight, and she is delivering it to me so we can have a romantic evening alone."

She chuckled. "She must really want you to date me."

"So, you'll come?" His heart sped up, even though he knew she would say yes. Just knowing he would have a whole evening with her made the future look bright. Dylan smiled. "You don't need to change."

She took a step back and held her arms out do while glancing down at her body. "Dylan, look at me right now. I know you said that you thought I looked beautiful but that doesn't change the fact that I'm wearing a wet swimsuit and sweatpants. I'm not exactly dressed for a nice dinner."

He glanced at the sky as if you were thinking deeply. Then he brought his gaze back down to Bonnie.

"Well, I think I have a solution. Maybe you should just take off the wet swimsuit when we get back to my place. Problem solved." He flashed a wink and a playful grin. "Naked eating is always good."

Bonnie laughed. "Tell you what. If you let me take a quick shower at your place and also let me borrow some more clothes of yours to wear, then we can head to your trailer now. I just want to get the pool off of me."

"Sounds like a deal." Dylan held his hand out to take Bonnie's and the two of them made their way back toward his place.

DYLAN LOVED WALKING ALONGSIDE BONNIE. He loved having her hand and her fingers interlocked with his. He noticed that his stride was a little longer and he held his chin a little higher when she was next to him. There was something about being in her presence that put him at ease. He had dated many women in his life, but none of them were like Bonnie. None of them had given him those butterflies of excitement in his belly that she did. There was something very special about her, and even though he couldn't put his finger on exactly what it was, he knew that she was worth cherishing and worth holding onto.

Maybe part of it is because she doesn't want me for my money, he thought. *It seems like Bonnie just enjoys spending time with me because she wants to spend time with me. There's a real connection here. I can feel it. I know for a fact it's not just in my imagination either.*

It was only a short walk back to his trailer, but in a way, he wished that it was a little bit further. He really enjoyed the simple things, and just strolling next to her put a smile on his face. He could see a future here.

"I think I can smell our dinner from here," he said, as they neared the trailer.

Bonnie drew in a long breath or her nostrils and nodded. "Me too. Smells amazing."

"Chef must have just dropped it off," he said. "Perfect timing."

They made their way down the dusty path that led to his home. As they stepped up onto the front porch, Dylan noticed a large brown paper bag that was stapled up at the top. On the front was a little smiley face drawn in black ink. Underneath it, the chef it scribbled the word "Enjoy."

"You really did have this all planned out, didn't you?" Bonnie said, squeezing Dylan's hand.

He glanced over at her and grinned. "I just wanted to do something special for you."

"Thank you, Dylan." She smiled, and his heart melted just a little bit more.

He picked up the brown paper bag and held open the door for her. She smiled again as she passed him.

Chef had followed his instructions perfectly. Not only had she made an amazing meal for the two of them, but she had also arranged his trailer to be as romantic as possible during her off time. The table in the dining room was arranged with three purple candles in the center. Next, to the candles, there was a bouquet of a dozen red roses. Playing throughout the speakers was soft classical music. He wanted to make sure this dinner was special for one reason, and that was because he thought that every dinner with Bonnie should be special.

She stopped in her tracks as soon as she saw the romantic set up. Then she turned around, her eyes wide with surprise. "You set all this up for me?"

Dylan smiled. "Technically, I asked Chef do it earlier, but I do have to take credit for the idea."

Bonnie approached him then stood on her tiptoes to give him a quick kiss on the lips.

"You are seriously the best," she said. "Nobody has ever done anything like this for me before. I feel so spoiled."

"Just wait," he said. "I actually have another surprise for you besides all of this."

"Are you serious?" She asked. She motioned to the candles and flowers. "Dylan, you've already done so much."

"I enjoy doing things for you," he said.

Her shoulders relaxed, and she smiled. It looked like she might cry.

"Thank you." Bonnie then placed her hands onto his forearms. She gave him a quick kiss. "Before we eat, can I get that shower that you promised me?"

"Of course," he said. "There's a change of clothes in the closet."

He watched her disappear through the doorway and into his room, then he headed upstairs to the guest bedroom to catch a quick shower of his own.

He stripped down and stepped into the shower. The whole time he was in there all he could think about was how excited he was about having Bonnie in his life.

Dylan knew that these were unique circumstances. Bonnie wasn't just some girl he had met in a bar and had decided to take home that night. The connection between them was so much more than that. She had confided in him, and he had told her that he could keep her safe. He needed her in his life, and he was going to do everything in his power to make that happen.

When he was done showering, he dried off and got dressed. He normally would have worn something nice for dinner with Bonnie, but since she was going to be wearing workout pants and a T-shirt, he decided to wear the same thing. Once dressed, he headed back downstairs to find Bonnie sitting at the dining room table wearing one of his t-shirts and pajama pants. Her hair was still a bit damp, making it appear darker than usual.

"Feel better?" He asked.

"Much better," she said. "Thank you. I needed that shower."

Dylan pulled the food from the oven and brought it over to the table, then took a seat across from Bonnie. He served up the chicken cacciatore and then filled the glasses with white wine.

He held his glass in the air. "We should do a cheers."

She nodded in agreement. "What should we cheers to, though?"

"How about we cheers to us?" He suggested.

"To us, huh?" She replied as she thought about it. "I like that. Here's to us."

They clinked their glasses together, and each took a sip.

Dylan was beside himself as he began to eat. He couldn't remember the last time he was this excited about a woman or this happy. For the first time in his life, he wasn't hesitant about the possibility of letting someone get close to him. He was ready to go all in with her, to throw caution to the wind. He was ready to open himself up to her more than he ever had for anyone before. All of this was related to the final surprise that he had for Bonnie that evening.

"How's the food?" he asked.

Bonnie finished a bite then swallowed it down with some wine. "It's *so* good! I can see why it's your favorite."

Dylan laughed. "Then we might have to make this a regular thing."

"I'd like that," she said, with a smile.

"Me too." He took a sip of wine and smirked at her. "Now all we have to do is convince Chef."

Bonnie laughed and raised her glass to cheers once again.

It was starting to get dark outside now. The sun had found its way behind the mountains and the sky was turning a dark shade of purple. The only light in the dining room was coming from the candles, surrounding them in a warm orange glow.

"This is really romantic, by the way," Bonnie said. "I'm glad you had Tyson ask to eat with friends. I love eating with him, but this is super nice."

Her eyes glowed in the candlelight, and her features became softer. She was already feminine, but this made her more desirable than Venus herself.

What Dylan really wanted to do right then was to clear the table and make love to Bonnie right then and there. It was tempting, but he wanted to give her the one last surprise first. He was a little nervous about it, and waiting would only make things worse.

"Are you ready for your surprise?" he asked, pushing the plates to the side.

She nodded eagerly. "Yes, please tell me. The suspense is killing me."

He went to the counter and picked up an envelope he had waiting there. "For you."

She carefully took the envelope from him and delicately opened it. Her eyes widened in surprise.

"These are plane tickets," she said. She looked up at him, not quite understanding.

"I want to take you to New Orleans," he explained. He sat down next to her, watching her face in the flickering candlelight. "I want to show you my home. I want to share it with you."

A slow smile filled her face. "You do?"

"Very much," he told her. "Please say you'll go."

She looked at the tickets in her hand and hesitated. "I have to ask Mia. And Mike."

"Mike?" He didn't know that name. Jealousy stirred in his belly.

She put her hand on his arm. "He's a police officer working my brother's case," she told him. The jealousy still swirled, and she must have seen it. "He's also ten years older than me and happily married."

"Oh. Okay." The jealousy ebbed. He shook himself to clear it. "Well, I can't speak for Mike, but I already asked Mia. She approved it."

"Of course you did," she said shaking her head. She smiled but didn't say yes.

"Will you come?" Anxiety started to creep up. He so wanted her to say yes. She paused and looked up at him.

"Yes." She grinned at him. "Yes, and thank you!"

Bonnie smiled, then wrapped her arms around his neck. She leaned over and brought her lips to his. She tasted sweet like the wine, and he reveled in her taste.

Bonnie broke the kiss. The expression on her face had changed. Her pupils dilated, and her eyes were dark. She licked her lips, and he noticed just how plump and perfect they were. How incredibly kissable.

"Let's go to the other room," she said, her voice husky with desire. Heat instantly flamed inside of him.

She then took his hand and let him down the center aisle of the trailer. Dylan happily followed.

As they entered the living room, he expected her to stop at the comfortable couch. She didn't do that, though.

Instead, she walked straight into the living room and into his bedroom. There was an urgency in her steps. She obviously had something on her mind, and Dylan hoped that she was thinking the same thing that he was.

As soon as they got into the room, Bonnie released his hand.

"Have a seat on the bed," she said.

He grinned. There was no way he was going to turn her down. She wanted the same thing he did, and he was already feeling his pants tighten as he watched her move. Her hips swayed, drawing him in like a magnet.

He took a seat on the edge of the bed and Bonnie approached him. She placed her hands on the top of his shoulders. He glanced up at her and noticed that she was gently biting her lower lip once again.

"Lay back," she said, the tone of her voice low and sexual. It made his brain go fuzzy with desire. All he could think about was having her. Bonnie gently pushed on his shoulders.

She leaned down and began kissing him again, only this time it was more than just their lips touching. Their tongues darted in and out of each other's mouths while Bonnie pressed her weight down over the top of him. The bulge under his sweatpants continued to grow until was pressing out firmly against the material. He could feel the warmth between her legs even though they were both still fully dressed.

Dylan's hands moved up her sides, taking the bottom of her shirt with them. Bonnie let out a soft moan the instant his fingers grazed her nipples. The sound made him so hard he nearly moaned himself.

Bonnie broke the kiss and sat up on Dylan's lap. He was still holding her shirt up, and her perfect breasts were exposed to him. She lifted her hands in the air, a smile on her face as if to give him permission to undress her. So he sat up and pulled her T-shirt off. As soon as he tossed it to the ground, he leaned in toward her chest and immediately began to pleasure her nipples with his mouth.

He couldn't get enough. The more he kissed her, the more he needed to kiss her. The more he touched her, the more he *wanted* to touch her. He breathed her soft scent in and pulled her close. The low sound of Bonnie's moans drove him wild.

He brought his gaze up and locked eyes with her. Before he could utter a sound, she leaned in and kissed him once again. It wasn't gentle, but instead full of such ferocious need that she pushed him back into the bed.

She rocked against his growing hardness, her head rolling back as she found pleasure from him, even though they were still clothed. He reached up, brushing a knuckle over the skin just under the swell of her breast. His finger traced southern, pausing to dance around her bellybutton.

She looked down, and her lower lip went between her teeth as he kept going lower. He slid his hand into the waistband of the pajama pants and found she wasn't wearing panties.

His eyes went to her, and she winked, giving him a sexy little shrug. It was a smile that promised all sorts of naughty pleasures.

His fingers searched for her pleasure spot, and he loved the way she gasped and arched her back as he found it. It was then that he flipped her onto the bed, her excited body giving him no resistance. He pulled off her pants, leaving her completely naked before him.

It was a feast of beauty, and his breath caught.

"You are so beautiful," he whispered, pulling his own

shirt off and tossing it to the floor before pressing his fingers into her again. He held her hip with one hand as he dragged his thumb over her. She panted with every brush, her eyes glassy with desire as he slowly tortured her with pleasure.

"Dylan," she gasped, her fingers digging into the bedsheets. "Please…"

Slowly, he slid a finger into her, followed by another. It was her undoing. She cried out, her back arching and the most beautiful expression of release filling her face as she bucked and writhed against his hand.

He nearly came just watching her. It was possibly the most erotic thing he'd ever seen to watch her come undone at his touch. To know that he had given her that pleasure. He kept the gentle touch of his thumb against her, keeping her lost to ecstasy for as long as possible.

Slowly, she came back to earth. His angle came back to him, her pupils blown and her mouth open as she sat up.

"I need you," she whispered. "I need more."

Her voice was husky with her orgasm. He vibrated with tension and knew he wouldn't last long if he didn't' have her as soon as physically possible.

He stood from the bed and pulled off his pants as he walked to the nightstand and removed a condom. His fingers were clumsy with the speed he wanted to get the condom on, but he managed to get it.

He straddled his beautiful creature on the bed. She looked up at him with dark eyes full of want for him.

"Please, Dylan…" Her breath came in small pants. "Don't make me wait."

So, he didn't.

He slid in deep and hard, feeling her heat and wetness take over him. His mouth found hers as he thrust deep again, her moans joining his. She threaded her hand through his dark hair, tugging him into her as she writhed her hips to give him better access to her.

He leaned back, putting both hands on her hips and thrusting home. The new angle was so deep, he nearly lost himself on the first thrust. She cried out, her hands grasping the sheets in a desperate attempt to control the pleasure coursing through her.

So deep, he pressed and heard a groan from deep inside of him. Release pulled at him, begging him to lose himself in this beautiful woman. He wanted to wait, to explore her further. He wanted to send her to pleasure a thousand times.

"Dylan, I need you," she whispered. Her eyes met his. "Make me yours."

Her words pushed him over the edge. He wanted her. Needed her. Desired her. He was as much hers, and she was his. His body claimed hers anyway.

Color exploded and sound faded. Everything but the sweet touch of her skin, the curve of her breast, and the smile on her face was lost to him. She was his everything. She was his.

He collapsed into her, pressing his forehead into the curve of her shoulder. Her arms and legs wrapped around him, pulling him into her. He never wanted to leave. He wanted to stay just like this forever. It would be heaven.

Slowly, their breathing returned to normal, and she released her death grip on him. He rolled to the side, and she cuddled into him. He loved the way she seemed to fit in the nook of his shoulder like she was built specifically for that spot.

"I think this was the best dinner of my life," she murmured. "And it had nothing to do with Chef's food."

He chuckled and kissed her forehead. "I agree."

She sighed with contentment and relaxed into him. This was heaven. He smiled, imagining a life for the two of them. Thoughts of having her with him always made his heart sing with possibilities and joy.

He smiled. The first step in their life together would be New Orleans. And she'd said yes.

Chapter 24

BONNIE STARED at her red duffle-bag and sighed. She was packing for their trip and was already done in less than two minutes. All of her clothes, the nice ones at least, were already packed. She had managed to find a skirt under one of the bags with her pictures albums in her trunk, but that was it.

She felt woefully under-dressed for the trip, but there wasn't much she could do about. The closest mall was almost an hour away, and she didn't feel comfortable with the idea of going to a crowded, public place like that. She wished she'd gone through with her idea to buy some clothes online.

Anxiety gripped at her throat. She took a deep breath and then started pacing her small room.

It was the trip. She was anxious about traveling. She

wanted to be with Dylan. That part of the trip she was looking forward to. She was looking forward to having him all to herself and the idea of sharing a hotel room.

No, it was the airport, the airplane, the city, the people. They were going to New Orleans. It was way further East than she wanted to go. It was a big city. There were people there that might say something to the Trio.

She'd called Detective Patton and told him she was going. She half wanted him to talk her out of it, but he said to go. The Trio didn't have a presence in New Orleans. As far as organized crime went, the Trio was small potatoes. It was why Brett's testimony was so important. They could shut down the Trio before they became a significant threat.

But, just because they were small didn't make them any less dangerous, just less likely to have agents in other cities.

She sighed and fiddled with the hairband on her wrist. She'd spent the last month avoiding big cities, and here she was packing to go to one. It felt weird. It felt dangerous.

Her burner phone began to buzz. Every time it rang, her stomach dropped and today was no different. If anything her stomach dropped further today.

The number displayed Detective Patton.

Her throat closed and she nearly dropped the phone. Worst case scenarios rushed through her mind. Her brother was dead. They'd found him. They'd found her. She had to run.

"Hello?"

"Hello, Bonnie. It's Patton." He sounded calm, but that was his default setting. "I wanted to be the one to tell you."

Her breath came in short gasps. "Tell me."

"The trial date's been set," Detective Patton informed her.

It took a moment for the words to sink in. It wasn't bad news. It was just news. Her brain stuttered to a stop, and she let out a giant sigh of relief. Her brother was fine.

"That's it?" she asked. Her legs gave out as she sat down hard on the bed. She had been ready for the worst.

"It'll be on the third," Patton replied. "You okay?"

"Yeah. Yeah." She nodded and lay back on the bed. Her heart was still jumping out of her skin like a cartoon character. "Do I need to be there?"

"No. In fact, I'd recommend you stay far, far away," the detective told her. "You aren't taking the stand, so we don't want you near it. Your brother will be fine. I know you'd like to give emotional support, but it's better if you stay safe."

"Okay." She closed her eyes and took a deep breath. "Thank you for letting me know. Is Brett doing okay?"

"He's great. He said to tell you that he's officially applying for the academy next year," Patton replied with a laugh. "I think he likes hanging out with cops all day."

She chuckled. "Watch, he'll get a job out of being a murder witness. That would be just like him."

"How are you doing?" Patton asked.

"I'm good." She meant it too. "I really like it here."

"Excited for your trip?" That was a loaded question.

"I'm a little nervous, but you said the Trio doesn't have a presence in New Orleans, so I'll be fine. Right?" She half wanted him to tell her to stay home.

"You should be," he told her, not really answering her question. "But stay on your guard. Now that the Trio has an end date, they have a deadline. They are going to push harder now."

"Should I cancel the trip?" she asked.

"You don't have to. Just be cautious. You said you're going

with Dylan Abbott, so that should be more than enough security," he replied. "If anything, you've got better security now than your brother does."

She looked over at the door of her cabin. She could see the blinking lights of the security system Dylan had installed for her and she knew there was a guard patrolling around her cabin. He promised even more security for their trip. She hoped it would be enough.

"Thank you, Mike." She felt safer knowing that her former neighbor and friend was watching her back. She hated needing someone else to make her feel safe. She would be glad when this was all over.

"Of course. You stay safe," he replied. "I'll call you if I get any other news. I know this isn't much, but it does mean that the end is in sight. You'll be able to come home soon."

I am home, she thought. It surprised her.

"Thank you again," she said instead. She clicked the phone off and set it on the bed beside her.

She didn't feel strong enough to get up, so she just kept her eyes closed as she lay on the bed. The world spun beneath her, and her fingers clung to the bedspread.

The trail was coming. Her brother would testify, and this would all be over. She could go home.

She swallowed hard. She didn't want to go home. She didn't want to leave Dylan.

Dylan. She was safe with him. She was home when she was with him.

She turned her head and looked at her packed bag. The idea of traveling away from this safe haven made her stomach go sour.

The trip was a bad idea. The trial date was set, and it put a deadline on finding her. They would be looking for her, and she was going to a big city. She didn't want to go. She wanted to stay here. She was safe here. She had a bad feeling about this.

She had to tell him no.

Chapter 25

Dylan

Dylan hadn't been this excited to visit his grandfather since he was a boy. He already had all the places he wanted to show Bonnie mapped out in his head. He wanted her to meet his grandfather. He wanted her to eat the food he remembered growing up. He wanted her to experience everything about the city that he loved.

He wanted to share his world with her.

Dylan had never brought another woman to New Orleans. His grandfather had never met any of his former girlfriends. It never felt right to introduce him to them. But, Dylan wanted his grandfather to meet Bonnie.

When he thought about what the meant, it made him both nervous and excited. He'd never felt this way about anyone before. He knew in his bones she was the one for him. They had amazing chemistry both in and out of the bedroom. She made him smile without trying.

He was head over heels in love with her.

He put the last couple things into his small carry-on bag. He didn't need much for the quick weekend trip, and if he did, it would be easy enough to buy things there.

Dylan felt light. His heart was happy and his world full of goodness. He was finally doing work that mattered to him. He was helping foster kids find their way in the world. He had a good woman that he was proud to introduce his grandfather to.

Life was good.

He grinned and headed out of his trailer to go pick up Bonnie for their flight. He opened the door and nearly tripped over her. She sat on the bottom step, her bottom lip between her teeth and her brow tight. Her dark eyes were deep and unhappy.

"What's wrong?" He dropped his bag and immediately sat down beside her.

She took a shaky breath. "I can't do this."

His heart dropped straight down to his toes. This? Them? He did his best to keep his voice calm and centered. "What do you mean?"

"I can't do this trip." She sniffled. "I'm so sorry."

He relaxed a little. It was the trip, not them. Being in a relationship that really mattered to him like this was new to him. He still had some things to get used to.

"Why?" He asked. He wanted her to go with him. He was so excited for her to meet his grandfather. This was important to him, but he wanted it to be important to her too. He wanted her to *want* to go.

"It's not safe," she told him.

"What?" He had taken all the precautions he and his security team could think of. He had the heads of security for three billionaires come up with the plan to keep her safe for the trip. The president of the United States had less security. "Where we're going is very safe. I wouldn't do anything to jeopardize your safety."

She sniffled and smiled at the same time. He had no idea what that meant.

"That's not it. It's not safe for me to go," she repeated.

He sighed. They'd been through this. They'd been through it several times. He understood that there were mobsters looking for her. He got that. He also understood that the Trio was a small organization that didn't have a lot of power anywhere but in her town.

Did she not realize how important this was to him?

"Bonnie, we've talked about this," he tried again. "We have enough security. You've seen what the heads of security came up with. You said it was enough."

He gently put his hand on her shoulder, and she pulled away hard. He tried to keep the hurt from her motion from showing.

"Things change," she snapped. She stood up, her arms wrapped around her.

"Bonnie, what's going on?" He kept his voice low and gentle. She was obviously upset about something. He didn't know what, but she needed him. The protective part of him wanted to wrap her up and punch anyone that came close to hurting her. He wanted to fix the world for her.

"They're looking for me," she whispered. "The trial's been set. If they can find me before the third, they'll be able to keep my brother from testifying."

He understood now. She was scared. She was pushing him away because she was terrified. His heart ached for her. The anger vanished instantly.

He got up and pulled her into his chest. This time, she didn't pull away. Instead, she tucked her head, burying her face in his shoulder. She shook like a leaf in the wind. He hated to see her this scared.

"I won't let anything happen to you," he whispered into her hair. "I promise."

"I'm just so scared," she admitted. "I'm scared for me. I'm scared for my brother. I just want this to be over. I'm so tired of looking over my shoulder all the time. I jump at every car that passes, even if I recognize them. I don't want to hide anymore."

He rubbed his hands along her back in slow, soothing circles as she cried into his shoulder. He wished he could make this better. He wished he had a secret crime-fighting alter ego that could go to New Jersey and wipe out the Trio. He wished he had some way, other than hiring security teams, to keep her safe.

But he didn't. He had hired the best security team money could buy to go with them. He had private tours and fake names all set up for the two of them. No one but his grandfather would even know they were in the city.

"Please come with me," he said softly once her breathing evened out. "I want you to meet my grandfather. I will keep you safe."

She sniffled.

"If you want, my grandfather can be the only person in the entire state of Louisiana that gets to see you," he offered. "I'll make everyone else leave."

She chuckled. "Having no one see me would make security hard. They should probably keep an eye on me."

He smiled. She was joking which meant she was feeling better. "You have a good point."

She pulled back and wiped at her face. Even blotchy from crying, she was still the most beautiful woman in the world to him.

"You promise you'll keep me safe?" she asked once more.

He smiled and kissed her forehead. "Extra security. Extra everything. I promise."

She nodded slowly. "You want me to meet your grandfather that badly?"

Embarrassment tugged at him. He hadn't told her how much this meant to him. "Yes. It's important to me. He's the reason I want to go. I want you to meet him."

She smiled at him. "He's important to you. It's important to you that I meet him?"

He nodded. "Yes. He's all I have left of my dad."

"So, this trip is really for me to basically meet your parents."

He shifted his feet. "More or less. You still need to meet my mom and my sister."

"I get the impression that you don't care what they think as much as you do your grandfather." Her brown eyes watched his face. How did she see him so easily?

"They like everyone. My grandfather is more... picky." There was a very good reason why he'd never brought a girl home to Grandfather. None of them measured up. He thought Bonnie would.

She hugged him. "I now see how important this is to you. So, let's go."

"Yeah?" His spirits lifted.

"Yeah. But, no public areas. I'm still not sure going to New Orleans is a great idea," she told him. "But, it's important to you. So, I'll go."

He grinned and hugged her.

She was going to meet his grandfather.

Chapter 26

 ylan

THE PLANE RIDE went smoother than Dylan could have hoped for. He knew she was nervous about flying and leaving their safe haven of the ranch. He wanted her to feel safe. Luckily, being a billionaire had some perks. Like private jets.

He'd loved watching her eyes go wide as they drove up to his jet. He'd loved watching her wander around the jet and asking if this was really all for them. He was fairly sure her mouth didn't close the entire take-off because she was so amazed to have the plane all to themselves.

That in itself made the purchase of the jet worth it.

They'd flown out of the small local airport. Carter had made sure the runway could handle jets, so the entire airport serviced only small crop dusters and multi-million dollar airplanes. It always made Dylan chuckle to see a ten thousand dollar crop duster sitting next to his ten million dollar jet on the tarmac like that was a normal thing.

The flight was quick and uneventful. She refused the champagne but loved the chocolate covered strawberries he'd had put on-board for her.

"Tell me about your grandfather," she said, settling into one of the over-sized white leather chairs. She popped a strawberry into her mouth.

"What do you want to know?" he asked, taking the seat opposite of her and grabbing his own strawberry.

She thought for a moment. "Your favorite memory of him."

"That's easy," Dylan told her. He smiled, remembering the moment. "I was nineteen and in college. I hated it. I hated going to classes that didn't matter and listening to professors that were only teaching because they couldn't get jobs in the field."

"Wow." Bonnie raised her eyebrows. "I sense no bitterness there."

He chuckled at her sarcasm. "I was supposed to get a finance degree so I could manage the family businesses. It wasn't what I wanted to do. I had this idea for a computer run business, but my dad was determined I would get this degree and that it would give me the best shot at a good future."

"You don't strike me as someone who would enjoy a finance degree," Bonnie replied.

He shook his head and made a sour face. "I hated it. I liked computers. I liked programming. I was really good at it too, but my father was insistent on the finance degree." Dylan shook his head slowly. "I wanted to tell him I was going to quit and do computer work, but I was terrified. I didn't want to disappoint him."

Bonnie nodded, taking another strawberry.

"It was Thanksgiving. We were all at my grandfather's house, per tradition. We'd already eaten, and I found myself out on the porch with PawPaw," Dylan continued. If he closed his eyes, he could still see it in his mind. The smell of leftover turkey and potatoes, the soft laughter of his mother and sister as they washed dishes, the cool breeze as it came in off the lake. It was all still fresh in his mind.

"Wait, you call your grandfather 'PawPaw?'" Bonnie asked, interrupting his memory.

"Yeah. What about it?"

She grinned. "It's cute. I love it. Go on."

He evaluated her for a moment before continuing. "Anyway, PawPaw and I were out on the porch, and he asked me how school was going. I almost told him it was great, and I was really enjoying it, but he put his hand on my shoulder, and I couldn't do it. I told him I hated it, and I wanted to quit, but I didn't want to crush my dad. I told PawPaw I had this idea for a computer tech company and I knew it was going to change the industry."

"How'd he react?" Bonnie's beautiful brown eyes watched him closely, taking in his story.

"He told me, 'Screw your dad. Do what makes you happy. You start that business.'" Dylan smiled at the memory.

"I think I like your PawPaw," Bonnie said with a nod.

"I was shocked. Family's important. Family is everything with my grandfather," he told her. "I couldn't believe it."

"Then what happened?" Bonnie asked.

"He wanted to know about my idea. He asked me all sorts of questions," Dylan replied. "After about an hour of me talking about it, he went to his office and came back with a check. He gave me two thousand dollars to start my business."

Bonnie's face softened with a sweet smile. "He did that?"

Dylan nodded. "He told me I could cash it as soon as I told my dad. And that I was to tell my dad that I already had an investor."

"What'd your dad say?" Bonnie asked, taking another strawberry.

"It took me until the next day to tell him," Dylan replied. "He was mad, but since I already had an investor, there wasn't much he could do about it. So, I finished the semester and then did my own thing."

"I'm guessing FirmHard Tech was your idea," Bonnie said. She looked around at the private jet. "I'd say your grandfather invested wisely."

Dylan chuckled and nodded. "My first and only investor. I think he's made his money back."

"I can't wait to meet him." Bonnie stood up from her chair and kisses his cheek. "Anyone who believes in you like that has to be an amazing person. Thank you for introducing us."

Dylan's heart swelled. He couldn't wait for PawPaw to meet her too.

THEY ARRIVED at another small airport north of his grandfather's house just as the sun was starting to set.

True to his word, he had security out the wazoo. He couldn't look around without seeing someone either in a suit or wearing plain clothes with an earpiece. Dylan had seen world trade meetings with less security.

He was going to keep Bonnie safe.

They took a limo to his grandfather's house. Again, her reaction to the limo made him smile. She loved playing the with various windows, music, lights, and features that he'd forgotten were novel.

It wasn't until they were a block away from his grandfather's house that he started to get nervous. He knew his grandfather would love Bonnie. He knew because Dylan loved her, and anything Dylan loved, so did his grandfather.

He was nervous because this was a big step for him. This truly meant that he loved her. This was the test to himself. He'd never brought anyone here because he'd never felt this way about anyone before. Bringing her to this place, the place he loved as a child, meant that it was real. That their relationship was a real thing.

The limo turned onto the road leading to the manor and Dylan started to sweat. He turned up the air and sat in front of the vent, doing his best to keep a calm face. He hadn't felt anywhere near this nervous during negotiations with Google for his company.

The limo came to a gentle stop in front of the house. Dylan waited patiently for the driver to open the door. Dylan stepped out first, wanting to see Bonnie's reaction to the house.

His feet crunched on gray pebbles as he stepped out. The humidity of the south hit him full in the face, warm and sweet. The scent of magnolias and night blooming jasmine drifted on the hot damp air. The hum of katydids, frogs, and the call of a whippoorwill called out like familiar friends saying hello.

He turned and offered Bonnie a hand to exit the limo. She stepped out with a grin.

First, she took a deep breath of the air, feeling the new

humidity and the heat. Her eyes went big, and her jaw dropped as she took in the home.

"Oh my, it's so pretty," she whispered, stepping away from the limo.

He smiled, feeling a little bit of his nerves calm. Meeting his grandfather was the real test, but the fact that she liked the house bode well.

He turned and looked at it with new eyes. It was as stereotypical southern plantation as he could imagine. Two stories with long, graceful white pillars and big porches wrapping around at perfect intervals made the house look suited to a Civil War documentary. Giant oak trees draped with Spanish moss flanked the white home.

The big center door opened, and yellow light poured out into the soft twilight as PawPaw came to greet them.

Dylan took a deep breath. It was time.

Chapter 27

$\mathcal{B}$onnie

BONNIE STOOD on the edge of the large front porch as Dylan embraced his grandfather. She waited politely, her hands clasped neatly in front of her as the two men greeted one another.

PawPaw was tall like his grandson. He had the same broad shoulders and lean frame, but where Dylan's hair was black, PawPaw's was silver. They had the same strong jaw and easy smile, but Dylan's eyes were darker. The family resemblance between PawPaw and Dylan was strong, which meant that Dylan would be a very attractive old man in fifty years.

"And you must be Bonnie," PawPaw said, releasing his grandson and stepping toward her. "I can't tell you how nice it is to meet you."

The man spoke with a soft southern drawl that Bonnie

found incredibly endearing. She shook his hand, and he grinned at her.

"It's very nice to meet you, sir," she told him. "Thank you for having us."

"Of course! Please come inside," he replied. "Would you like some lemonade? Milly makes the best lemonade I've ever had."

He offered her his arm like a true southern gentleman to escort her inside. Bonnie grinned and looked back at Dylan.

"Milly really does make the best lemonade in the whole city," Dylan told her. "I'll get the bags."

She took PawPaw's arm, and he led her inside the house. It was just as cozy on the inside as it was beautiful on the outside. She walked across a beautiful marble entrance, feeling like she should be wearing a hoop skirt and big southern bonnet. The marble gave way to wood floors and simple, yet elegant furniture. It felt grand and welcoming at the same time.

They made their way to the kitchen. Black and white tiled floors and white appliances dominated the space, and there was a large wooden table next to a big window overlooking a garden. It was possibly the most beautiful kitchen Bonnie had ever seen.

Mr. Abbott dropped her off at the kitchen table, pulling out a wooden chair for her to sit on before going to the refrigerator and taking out a glass pitcher. He carefully poured two glasses and joined her at the table.

"So, you're the woman who has stolen my grandson's heart," he said, handing her a glass.

"What?" She was glad she hadn't tasted her drink yet because she nearly choked on her own breath. "What makes you say that?"

She did like the way it made her heart swell to hear it.

Dylan had certainly stolen her heart, but she wasn't sure she had his. He was, after all, a billionaire that could have anyone.

Mr. Abbott chuckled. "You're the first girl he's brought here," the man told her.

"I can't be the first girl he's brought," Bonnie replied, shaking her head. She had a hard time believing she was that special.

Mr. Abbott just sipped his lemonade and shrugged.

"Really?" she asked.

Mr. Abbot chuckled and reached across the table to pat her hand. "He tells me you're a teacher," he said, changing the subject to something she was more comfortable with.

"Yes, yes I am," she replied. She suddenly felt very nervous. She hoped she could live up to PawPaw's expectations. She wanted to make Dylan proud. "I'm a special education teacher."

"That means you have patience and can deal with his stubbornness," he replied. He motioned to her untouched glass. "Try the lemonade."

"Oh, of course." She quickly took a sip. The sour of lemon and the sweetness of sugar hit her tongue in perfect harmony. "Oh, my. This is amazing."

"Milly won't tell me the recipe, but I think she uses honey *and* sugar." He took a long sip and smacked his lips. His eyes went to hers. They were a lighter than Dylan's but had the same dark warmth that she found intriguing. "Do you love him?"

He luckily asked the question after she finished swallowing her sip of lemonade. As it was, she still had to set her glass down and take a moment to compose herself.

"I think I do," she replied honestly, her eyes on her glass of lemonade. "We haven't known each other for very long, but he makes me very happy. I've never met anyone who makes me as stupid giddy-happy as he does." She looked up from the table at him and shrugged. "Does that answer your question?"

Mr. Abbott gave her an appraising look, his dark eyes thoughtful. He didn't say anything, just sipped on his lemonade.

"My ears are burning," Dylan announced, walking into the kitchen. He got himself a glass and poured his own lemonade. "Were you two talking about me?"

"Wouldn't you like to know?" his grandfather teased. He smiled at Bonnie and gave her a friendly wink.

"Tell Milly her lemonade is still as delicious as always," Dylan said, setting his empty glass on the counter. He looked over at Bonnie. "Milly is PawPaw's housekeeper."

"She keeps me in line," Mr. Abbott agreed. He stood up from the table. "Well, I know that Dylan has a wonderful supper planned for you this evening. I'm going to get my old bones to bed."

"Oh? You aren't joining us?" Bonnie asked, rising from the table as well.

Mr. Abbott smiled and patted her arm as he came around. "Thank you, darling, but no."

"Thank you for the lemonade, Mr. Abbott," Bonnie replied, trying to think of all the manners her mother had tried to teach her. "I hope we'll see you in the morning."

"Call me PawPaw," Mr. Abbott told her with a smile. "And it's my pleasure to have you here."

He patted her arm and then headed off to the stairs to go to bed.

"He didn't give you too much grief, did he?" Dylan asked once his grandfather had left the kitchen. "He can be a little crusty sometimes."

"He's wonderful," Bonnie assured him. "He obviously loves you very much."

"Well, what's not to love?" Dylan asked, indicating to himself. She laughed, and he grinned. "Would you like some dinner?"

"I would love some, but could I freshen up first?" Bonnie looked down at her shirt to see she'd spilled some lemonade on her front. She sure was classy sometimes.

"Of course," Dylan said. "Let me show you to your room."

He took her up the grand staircase and down a large hallway full of beautiful paintings. Bonnie hoped she'd have time to explore the house during the daytime.

"This is your room," Dylan said, pointing to the first door on the left.

"Okay," she said. "Where's your room?"

"Right across the hall," he replied, motioning behind him. "And PawPaw is all the way at the end of the hallway. Plus, he's a deep sleeper."

Bonnie shook her head but grinned at him. "You're naughty."

"You like it," he replied. He kissed her cheek. "Come downstairs when you're ready. There's something in the bedroom for you."

She looked up at him, and he grinned before going into his own room. She smiled and went to open her door.

The room was made for a princess. Two French doors stood open to a balcony overlooking the back gardens. The sounds of twilight filled the air, and the scent of magnolias filled the room. She looked over at the beautiful canopy bed and saw a brand new dress laying out for her.

She fingered the soft fabric. Bright red cherries covered the simple A-line pattern. It looked adorable and incredibly southern to her eyes. She loved it. It was the perfect dress for the evening.

She went to the bathroom and cleaned up before coming back out to put on the dress. The bathroom was just as lavish and beautiful as the bedroom.

I could get used to this, she thought to herself as she slid the soft dress over her shoulders. The dress fit perfectly. It shaped her hips and hugged in the right places. She couldn't have picked a better dress if she'd tried.

She fixed her hair and makeup and went downstairs, feeling like a princess meeting her prince charming.

Chapter 28

onnie

BONNIE DESCENDED the beautiful grand staircase and felt as regal as Scarlett O'Hara meeting Rhett Butler. Dylan waited for her at the bottom of the stairs, his eyes on her as she came down, step by step. He wore dark dress pants and a dark gray dress shirt that showed off his shoulders and trim waist. He looked good enough to eat.

"Wow," he said as held out his hand for her. "You look beyond amazing."

She grinned. "You have good taste," she told him. "Thank you for the dress."

"My pleasure," he replied, holding out his arm. "This way to dinner."

She rested her hand on his forearm as they walked. She could get used to this, she decided. She could get used to an elegant life with him. They stepped outside and into what

Bonnie would classify as the backyard, but it was less back-yard and more magical fairy garden.

A small stone fountain gurgled in the center with neat paving stones leading off into different paths. The scent of magnolias was thick on the humid air, and the hum of insects and birds were music. She didn't feel hot though. It was the perfect temperature to sit out and drink something cold.

Dylan guided her to a small table and chairs set off to the side. White linen tablecloths with white china and polished silver sat waiting with two flickering candles as accents. Dylan pulled out her chair like a true southern gentleman before sitting himself.

"This is beautiful," Bonnie whispered, looking around the garden. Everything was lush and green. The hum of insects filled the air, but none buzzed around her. She suspected Dylan had something nearby to repel them and keep their evening comfortable.

"So, tonight's meal is all my favorite foods from New Orleans," Dylan told her. "I hope you like them."

"I'm sure I will love them," she assured him. "You haven't given me a bad meal yet."

He grinned. "First up, oysters Rockefeller."

A man in a waiter's uniform came up to their table and carefully deposited a large silver tray in the center for the two of them to split. He then poured each of them a glass of wine.

"Wow." Bonnie took a sip of her wine and watched the waiter. "You really went all out."

Dylan shrugged. "It was fun to set up. Now, try them. I'm curious to see what do you think."

She reached for an oyster shell. It smelled amazing, even if it looked a little strange and green. She used her fork to put the oyster in her mouth and sighed with pleasure. The oyster was baked in butter and covered in what Bonnie suspected was breadcrumbs and herbs. It melted in her mouth with richness.

"That's delicious," she said, reaching for another.

Dylan grinned. "A New Orleans restaurant came up with them over a hundred years ago. They were so rich, they had to be named after the richest man at the time." He reached for one of the half shells. "Thus, oysters Rockefeller."

"They are amazing," she said, happily taking another half shell. "I don't usually go for oysters, but these are really good."

"I'm glad you like them," he replied, a pleased grin filling his face as he watched her enjoy the food.

She paused. "Are you trying to seduce me, Dylan Abbott?" she asked. "I mean, oysters are an aphrodisiac."

"Maybe," he replied with a confident grin. "And we're only on the appetizer."

She laughed and reached for another.

"You ate this growing up?" she asked, as they finished off the plate of oysters. "This doesn't seem like kid food."

"I didn't like these until I was in high school," Dylan admitted. "We would come out here for Thanksgiving and Christmas. My dad would pick up oysters at the market on our way here just for PawPaw to make these. They always make me think of holidays now."

Bonnie watched as Dylan's eyes went distant with the memory of his father.

"You miss him," she said softly. Dylan's dark eyes came back to her.

"Yes." He sighed. "We butted heads a fair amount, but he was a good dad. He just wanted the best for me."

"Is he the one who taught you how to work on cars?" she

asked, sipping her wine. It was light and complimented the oysters well.

Dylan nodded. "It was the one thing we could always agree on. He was always fixing up junkers and mending the farm equipment. I loved to help him. He taught me everything I know about cars."

Bonnie could just imagine a small Dylan with his hands in the engine helping his father. The dark eyes bright with excitement and the nimble fingers learning the parts. It made her smile.

"Is that how you met Carter Williamson?" Bonnie asked. "I am a little curious how you became friends with the man who owns W Motors."

Dylan chuckled. "We billionaires have to stick together," he replied. "It's a tough world out there for us."

"Oh, I'm sure," Bonnie agreed as the waiter returned and filled their glasses. "Those gold plated jets don't buy themselves."

Dylan chuckled.

"I bought one of the first versions of his electric cars, and he wanted my feedback," Dylan explained. He smiled at the memory. "We talked cars for a good two hours without realizing it. Our secretaries were not pleased."

"Dinner, sir." The waiter placed two bowls in front of each of them before bowing away.

"Oh, this smells so good." Bonnie started to drool.

The bowl before her wasn't fancy. It looked rather simple, but it smelled absolutely heavenly. Bonnie knew what it was from their dinner on the overlook. Jambalaya.

"This is my grandfather's secret recipe," Dylan told her. "I asked him to make it for us tonight. You won't find better in the entire city."

Bonnie grinned and dug in. Spicy and savory flavors

filled her mouth. The simple ingredients blended to perfection in her mouth. Rice, shrimp, sausage, celery, peppers, and seasonings all were cooked to perfection. She could see why Dylan loved this meal. She felt honored that he'd shared it with her.

"My brother would love this," she said, barely pausing long enough to get the words out before taking another bite.

"Yeah?" Dylan looked up.

"He loves spicy," she replied with a smile. She looked around. "Actually, I think he'd love this place."

"I can't wait to meet him," Dylan replied.

Bonnie swallowed hard. That meant future. She looked up and found herself wanting her brother to meet Dylan. She wanted to have Christmas here with the two of them and PawPaw. She could see a whole future where the two men of her life were friends.

She wanted it.

"Once the trial's over, I want you to meet him." It felt good to say the words. "I wish you could meet him now. He's not a car guy, but I think you two would get along."

"What do you plan on doing after the trial?" Dylan asked. She noticed how he paused, as if afraid of her answer.

She looked down at her plate. It was empty.

"I'm not really sure," she said slowly. She looked up and into his eyes. They were dark in the twilight, but the candle-light made them sparkle. Her heart sped up, and she knew her answer just by looking at him. "I want to stay with you."

She loved the slow smile that filled his handsome face. She loved the way his dark eyes lightened with joy.

"I'd like that very much." He reached out and took her hand. His touch was gentle, yet it gave her strength.

The waiter cleared his throat once they'd had their quiet moment.

"Dessert, sir. Ma'am." He had two beautiful plates that looked more like art than dessert. He carefully set them down, handed Dylan a lighter, and then disappeared back into the darkness of the garden.

"Dessert is my favorite," Dylan announced. "Beignets and bananas foster."

Dylan flicked the lighter to life and lit the bananas on fire. Bonnie shrieked with surprise and delight as the flames reached into the night. The flames receded, leaving the most amazing aroma.

She carefully put some of the flambeed bananas on a plate and added one of the square doughnuts to the side. It was heaven on a plate. Sugar, sweet, and delicious.

"Your grandfather said that I'm the first girl you've brought home," she said after a moment.

She loved that his cheeks darkened. He set down his beignet. "Yes. Well, other than my high school girlfriend who came to Thanksgiving."

"Sounds serious," she teased. "Do I need to be worried?"

He shrugged and finished his beignet. "We did date for three months, which is basically forever in high school."

She nodded, finishing her own beignet. "So, I *should* be worried."

He reached over and wiped some powdered sugar from her cheek. "Very."

She loved the way her body heated when he touched her. She loved the goosebumps that popped up when he said her name.

"Well, maybe I can help you forget her," she said. With him touching her skin, she wasn't interested in dessert anymore, no matter how delicious it was.

"Yeah?" His voice deepened and the crooked sexy smile

she couldn't get enough of filled his face. "I might know a way."

She grinned and grabbed his hand. "Show me."

Together they disappeared from the garden and ran laughing up to Dylan's bedroom.

Chapter 29

BONNIE TIPTOED down the hallway to Dylan's room. She felt like a teenager again, sneaking past her parents to meet the love of her life. Only this time, she really was with the love of her life.

"You know he can't hear you," Dylan said, opening up the door to his room. "That door is solid, plus he sleeps with a white noise machine on. Nothing wakes him up."

"Don't spoil my fun," she replied. "I'm being sneaky."

He chuckled and together they went into his room. Where Bonnie's room was delicate and feminine, Dylan's was masculine and nautical. It had the same French doors leading out to a balcony, and the bathroom was similar, but it was much more male. It suited him.

"This was always my room as a kid," Dylan explained. For a moment he looked small and innocent before returning to the powerful man Bonnie knew.

"You ever think you'd bring a girl up here?" she asked, looking around. She went to the French doors and opened them up. The magnolia-scented breeze was heavenly if a little warm. She could see over the garden and out into the acres of land. Everything was gilded in the moonlight and almost surreal with beauty.

"I hoped," he told her. He joined her out on the balcony. "Never got quite this far."

"Well, I hope I don't get you in trouble," she said, making her voice breathy and sensual.

"Oh, we wouldn't want that," he agreed, pulling her to him.

He kissed her, igniting the flame low in her belly. She arched against him, eliciting a rough groan from deep within his chest. The reverberations only fed the flames inside of her.

"You're far too overdressed," he complained, tugging at the straps of her dress. She shimmied out of it without protest, barely breaking the kiss. He undid the buttons on his shirt and took it off.

The air was warm against her skin. It felt good to be naked in the humid twilight. Moonlight shone down on them, making everything glow with its magic.

She couldn't stop touching him. The moment she paused and looked up at him, she lost her breath. His tanned skin displayed every toned muscle to perfection. His eyes met hers, dark and hungry.

His mouth covered hers again and she lost herself to the feel of his skin against hers. He dipped his head and slid his lips down her throat. Every nerve ignited with his touch, driving her wild. Every touch, every kiss made her frantic for more.

His fingers worked at her bra, finally managing the

straps and pulling it free. She loved the male noise of appreciation as his hands cupped her breasts. His rough fingers teased her nipples before sliding down and holding onto the bare skin of her hips.

He didn't stop there. He hooked his nimble fingers on the lace of her panties and tugged. She kicked them free once they were around her ankles.

"Your turn," she told him, her hands already at his waist and working the button on his pants. He gently moved her hands and undid the buttons. She was grateful that he could do it so much faster since they were his own.

He stood there in the moonlight, naked before her and she lost her breath. There was no one for miles, yet being outside in the night air had a delicious naughtiness that only added to the play of before. They were being sneaky and bad.

She loved it.

"Bonnie." He said her name again, his voice strained with desire as he looked at her. She'd never felt so sexy in her entire life. Dylan could make any woman with a pulse feel sexy, but she also felt safe with him. Sexy and safe. It was a heady combination.

He reached for her, threading his hands through her hair as he kissed her. She tipped her face up to meet his, finding his lips and tongue. He was delicious. Everything about him tasted and felt good. His hands roamed down her sides, down to her backside, pulling her into him. She could feel how hard and excited he was.

If that didn't make her feel wanted, nothing would.

She raised her leg, lifting it to wrap around him. She felt him surge against her, seeking entrance. He was nearly home free, and she wanted him inside of her. She needed him to complete her.

He knew what to do. Without letting her go, he slid into place. She sighed with contentment, then moaned as he filled her to depth she didn't know she possessed. He plunged into her, and she held onto him for dear life. Every moment was a step toward heaven.

She couldn't hold the position for long, though. As much as she wanted to be a sex goddess, she was only human and her balance only decent. She had a better idea, though.

She dropped her leg and stepped back, giving him a coy smile as she walked to the balcony. She carefully placed both hands on the white iron railing and then looked over her shoulder. His eyes dilated, and she could have sworn he started to drool.

His body was hot against hers as he found his way back to her. His heat and the New Orleans' summer was enough to give her a fever. She moaned softly as he filled her, merging his heat with hers. The soft, warm breeze danced over the two of them.

Her knuckles went white as she lost herself to the pleasure only he could give her. He controlled their movements, and he knew what he was doing. Every motion, every inch was a little bit of heaven.

"Bonnie," he growled, his voice primal.

"Do it," she gasped. She was on birth control. She trusted him. She wanted this.

Together they flew. Together they flew over the edge into complete pleasure, losing themselves and finding the other. Everything merged. Everything was perfect for an indescribable moment of bliss.

Her knees were weak as she came down off her high. Dylan wrapped his arm around her, holding her up as much as keeping himself steady. He was her anchor in a spinning world of wonderful over-stimulation.

"You kill me," he whispered, his breathing rough as he bent his head to her back. She stood up slowly and turned to face him.

His eyes were bright in the moonlight. Sweat glistened on his skin as his chest muscles flexed with every breath. She had thought she was satisfied a moment ago, but seeing him like this revved her engine to maximum yet again.

"You're not dead yet," she told him, taking his hand. "But I'm going to send you to heaven anyway."

She led him back into the bedroom and dropped him off at the bed.

"Again?" he asked. He looked surprised and pleased at the same time.

"I guess those oysters worked," she teased. "I plan on enjoying you just as much. We have all night."

She knelt on the bed and licked her lips before leaning over him. She wanted to taste him now.

"I knew you'd like the food here," he said, groaning as she did just that.

Chapter 30

onnie

BONNIE WOKE up the next morning to the smell of freshly brewed coffee. She was perfectly comfortable and didn't want to move. At the same time, though, the idea of coffee sounded pretty amazing.

After a while, she finally opened her eyes. The sun was pouring in through the bedroom window, brightly illuminating the room.

It must be late morning, she thought. *That's weird. I never sleep in. Am I actually feeling relaxed for once, that my mind let me catch some much-needed sleep? If no, then this vacation is already the best thing I've done for myself in years.*

She glanced over to the opposite side of the bed where Dylan had slept that night. He wasn't there, though. However, there was something in his place.

Bonnie kicked off the covers and reached over to the other side of the bed. Folded neatly on top of the blanket was a beautiful sundress. She picked it up and let it unfold in front of her.

The blue fabric was soft and light- perfect for a day out in the New Orleans' heat. There was a flowery pattern stitched into the material of the dress, and by the look of it, it was hand-stitched. It was even prettier than the one from the night before.

A small piece of paper had fallen out of the dress, and she noticed it for the first time. She picked it up and read what was scribbled in black ink.

Good morning, Beautiful. I hope you slept well. I also hope you like your new dress. Come downstairs when you wake up. I have lots more surprises for you today.

SHE GRINNED as she read the note as she held the dress. He knew she didn't have many clothes since she was on the run and living out of her car. The beautiful dresses he had given her were such perfect gifts. She couldn't wait to thank him.

Bonnie got out of bed and headed to the bathroom to take a quick shower. She figured that she might as well get ready for the day before heading downstairs. Plus, she really wanted to try on the new dress and show it off to Dylan right away.

She turned on the shower and stepped into the hot water. She could still smell the coffee wafting all the way from downstairs, and enjoying a cup of it sounded better and better. She'd heard wonderful things about the chicory coffee that New Orleans was famous for. She couldn't wait to try it.

After her shower, she dried her hair then quickly got dressed. As soon as she pulled the summer dress up onto her shoulders, she walked over to the large mirror in the bathroom. Her smile widened the moment she saw herself in it. It was officially one of the most beautiful dresses she had ever tried on. It fit her perfectly. It seemed to hide the curves of her body that she hated and accentuated the ones that she loved. She couldn't wait to wear it on whatever adventures Dylan had planned for that day.

A quick check on her phone showed a message from Mia. For a moment, her heart sank, thinking something might be wrong. When she opened it up, a beaming picture of little Tyson filled her screen. "Someone just wanted to let you know that he missed you." It made her smile, and she quickly sent a message back saying that she and Dylan both missed him as well.

Dylan and his grandfather were downstairs talking in the kitchen. She could hear them speak, but couldn't make out what they were saying. It was mostly their laughing that caught her attention, though. Something about hearing that made her feel calm. It reminded her when she was younger, and she'd wake up early to hear her parents chatting over coffee in the morning. Something about it was nostalgic.

After taking one last look in the mirror, Bonnie headed downstairs. When she turned the corner into the kitchen, she saw Dylan and his grandfather sitting at the round, white table at the far end of the kitchen. They sat next to each other, with the newspaper opened up in front of them on the table. Both of them had a cup of coffee in their hand, and they were laughing to themselves as they read something in the paper.

"They're going to make it to the series, PawPaw," Dylan said. "They're a hell of a team. Ever since they got that new pitcher, they've been unstoppable."

"I can't believe it," PawPaw said, shaking his head. "Well, it's nice to see the underdog team have a chance. That's all I can say."

Bonnie took another step further toward them and cleared her throat. Both of the men looked up from their newspaper. Dylan's eyes widened the moment that he saw Bonnie.

"Good morning, Beautiful," Dylan said, standing up from his seat. "I see you found the dress."

"Yes, and what you think?" she asked while twirling around once to show it off to them.

"I think you look amazing." Dylan approached her and pulled her in for a hug, giving her a quick peck on the cheek before releasing her.

"You look cute as a button," PawPaw said to Bonnie. "In fact, I'd say are the prettiest girl this side of the Mississippi. Although, I do wonder something."

"What's that?" Bonnie asked.

"Should I be proud or should I be concerned at how good Dylan is at picking out dresses?" PawPaw said, with a mischievous grin.

His comment made Bonnie laugh out loud.

"Very funny, PawPaw," Dylan said, with a chuckle. "I promise that I'm not good at picking out dresses. It's just that Bonnie makes anything look good."

"Thank you," Bonnie said, her cheeks tingling as she blushed from the comment. "I love the dress, Dylan."

"Come join us for breakfast," PawPaw said, motioning Bonnie over to the table. "Have a cup of chicory with us before you head out for the day."

"That sounds great," Bonnie said. "I've heard good things about chicory coffee."

She sat down next to the old man, while Dylan fixed everyone a fresh cup of the coffee and chicory blend. He wore a white button-down shirt with gray slacks that accentuated his trim figure. He had the cuffs rolled up on the shirtsleeves, displaying his strong forearms.

"What do you two have planned for the day?" PawPaw asked as he patted the top of Bonnie's hand, just like her own grandfather used to do.

"It's a surprise," Dylan said, setting the coffee down onto the table. He put out some scones and muffins for Bonnie as well. "I've got some fun things planned for us, though."

"When you guys get back, we can all sit around and tell embarrassing stories about Dylan from when he was a kid." PawPaw flashed a wink.

"You promise?" Bonnie asked, peeling open a muffin and taking a bite. "Because I'd like to hear some of those."

"Trust me," Dylan said. "You don't want to hear *any* of those."

"When he was seven years old, he decided to run away from home," PawPaw began.

"And we're going to be late if we don't get going," Dylan interrupted, making PawPaw laugh.

"Let the lady finish her muffin," PawPaw chastised, but he had a grin on his face.

"So, Dylan was running away from home?" Bonnie prompted. Dylan made a sour face at her, which she just grinned at.

"Yes. He was darn determined, too. He'd just been told he was getting a little sister," PawPaw told her. "He packed up his backpack with everything he thought he'd need. He had apple juice, some cheese crackers, bug spray, and his teddy bear."

"Dylan had a teddy bear?" Bonnie asked, grinning as she ate her muffin.

"His name was Frank," PawPaw informed her. "He got as far as Elm Street before he decided that living with PawPaw was a better option. So, he came straight back and told his mother he was no longer running away, but instead, he was going to live with me. They could keep his sister."

"Mom was not pleased," Dylan said, taking a sip of coffee. "Dad thought it was hilarious."

"But now you and your sister get along just fine," PawPaw replied. He nodded as he spoke. "He was a good kid."

"I can believe that." Bonnie smiled at the two of them. "So, what's my surprise, Dylan?"

Dylan grinned. "You're just going to have to come with me to find out."

"Happily," she agreed. "PawPaw, are you coming with us?"

"Not today," he said. "I'm in charge of dinner. You two be home on time. I'm making étouffée. It's one of Dylan's favorites."

"PawPaw makes the best in the whole world," Dylan agreed. "I'm already looking forward to it."

"I can't wait," Bonnie assured him. She was looking forward to dinner now, too. "Thank you for breakfast."

The older man smiled, looking remarkably like his grandson. "You are most welcome."

"Thanks, PawPaw," Dylan said, standing from the table. "We'll be back in a bit."

PawPaw nodded and sipped at his coffee as Bonnie and Dylan got up and headed out the front door. A limo was waiting for them outside. Bonnie was glad to see the windows were tinted and impossible to see inside. The driver hopped out and held the door open for the two of them.

"Where are we going?" Bonnie asked, settling herself in the limo. She still wasn't used to being shuttled around in such a fancy car. She knew that Dylan had driven her in a more expensive car, but somehow the limo felt more extravagant.

"We're going to see the city," Dylan informed her.

"Dylan, I can't." Frustration started to form, and she lost her smile. "I can't go into the city."

"No one will see you, I guarantee it," he told her with a grin.

She was curious now. She crossed her arms but leaned back in her seat. "How?"

"Because we're going by helicopter." He grinned.

"Helicopter?" Her arms fell as Dylan nodded.

"Private helicopter and then an airboat ride," he told her. "You'll get to see the city without ever setting foot in a crowd. Then we'll see some 'gators."

Bonnie leaned over and kissed him. He had found a way to show her the city he loved without putting her at risk. She would be able to see New Orleans and without fear of being seen by the Trio.

"Thank you," she whispered. "Thank you for this."

He grinned. "Just wait until dinner."

THE CRESCENT CITY WAS BEAUTIFUL. The way the Mississippi wound through the city, the beautiful old buildings and even the city skyline were all breathtaking. Bonnie felt like she really did get to have a taste of New Orleans as they flew through the city.

The helicopter was so much fun. She'd never been in one before, and she vastly preferred it to a plane, even Dylan's private jet. She loved being able to hover over something and really be able to get a good look.

She couldn't wait until she could come back and explore the city on foot after the trial. There were so many places that she wanted to see the inside of, and she wanted to meet the people dancing on the street and throwing beads at tourists.

The helicopter didn't bring them back to the airport. Instead, it brought them out into the deep bayou where an air-boat was waiting to take them. Dylan greeted the captain and introduced him to Bonnie.

"So, how does this work?" Bonnie asked, climbing into the boat. The boat was small with just two seats and a captain's chair behind them. A giant fan sat on the back of the boat.

"Have a seat, and I'll show you," Captain Lafayette told her. He handed her a headset once she was settled next to Dylan in the two chairs.

The engine roared to life, and suddenly Bonnie understood the need for the headsets. The sound of the fan vibrated through the entire boat.

"This engine allows us to go in shallow water a normal boat engine can't go in," Captain Lafayette explained through the headset. She was impressed that he'd answered her question without her having to ask it. "There's no operating parts under the water, so we don't have to worry about getting stuck."

He pulled the boat out onto the river. The sky was crystal blue, and the bayou was calling them. Dark trees covered in Spanish moss rose out of the murky edges of the river to greet them. Herons flew overhead and everywhere Bonnie looked there was life.

"Look over there," Dylan said through the headset. He pointed at the river bank where a massive alligator slowly lumbered into the water. Bonnie's jaw dropped. She hadn't expected to see one that big this close to civilization.

Bonnie settled in and watched the river transform into life. The river was green and brown, and then it meandered off into the trees. Everywhere she looked, she could see birds, turtles, alligators, and fish. She didn't know just how alive the bayou was until that very moment.

It was stunning, and Bonnie could see exactly why Dylan loved this place.

She loved PawPaw and his relationship with Dylan. She knew she was special since Dylan was choosing to share the person he respected most with her. She knew it was love.

She reached over and took his hand. He looked up from the water and grinned at her. Hope shone in his eyes as she smiled back. He was showing her his world. It meant everything to her. This was what was important to him and being out here meant more to her than any gaudy trip to LA or New York City ever could.

Chapter 31

B onnie was sad to leave. She loved this house. She loved PawPaw's hospitality. She loved how Dylan shared his childhood with her and the way he smiled at everything. She was happy here. She felt almost as safe here as she did at the ranch.

But, she wanted to get home. They were still too close to the city for her to feel comfortable. Dylan had made sure there was plenty of security, and while they did blend into the background, she could always tell that they were there. She saw them out of the corner of her eye and would startle until she realized they were security and not intruders.

"Thank you so much for having us," Bonnie told PawPaw as the limousine drove up to get them. "I hope you'll come out and visit us sometime soon."

PawPaw wrapped her up in a big bear hug and squeezed.

"I'd love that. You know you're invited out here for Thanksgiving, right?"

"I wouldn't miss it for the world," she assured him. PawPaw grinned before turning to Dylan.

"This one's a keeper," PawPaw told him.

"I already knew that," Dylan replied, but he beamed with pride. PawPaw hugged his grandson.

The limo pulled to a stop, and Dylan helped PawPaw put their things in the trunk before one more round of goodbyes. PawPaw stood on the porch, waving goodbye as they drove away. Bonnie opened the window and waved for as long as she could before the limo turned, and PawPaw was obscured by the trees.

"Thank you for bringing me here," she said softly, rolling up her window. The air conditioning felt cold after the heat of the sunshine. Even though it was still early in the day, the New Orleans' southern heat was rising.

"Thank you for coming," he replied. Dylan leaned over and kissed her cheek, making her smile.

She watched as they drove, taking in the sights. The big oak trees covered in Spanish moss were so different than the big pines of home. With a start, she realized that she now thought of Colorado as home, rather than New Jersey.

She looked over at Dylan as he too watched the world out the window. It wasn't Colorado that was home. It was Dylan. Where ever he was, that was home.

The limo came to a stop just outside the tarmac of the small airport. It was larger and busier than the one in Silver Springs. Several people with suitcases walked along the sidewalk. Most were busy talking into cell phones or checking their departure times, but it made her uneasy. There were a lot of eyes here.

"You're just being paranoid," she told herself as the

driver opened the door. She wished she'd remembered to bring her sunglasses with her in the limo, but they were packed in her bag. She felt very exposed all of the sudden.

She stepped to the side and opened up her carry-on bag from the trunk. She wanted the sunglasses for the quick walk to their plane. She had a horrible sensation that something was about to happen. She needed to hide.

"Are you okay?" Dylan asked, putting his hand on her shoulder.

"I just need some sunglasses," she replied. She couldn't find them. They had to be in the bag somewhere.

"Okay. We can wait," he replied. "Do you want mine?"

"No, that's okay, I'll find them in just a second," she replied digging further into her bag. Her fingers felt the curve of plastic, and she sighed with relief as she pulled them out. They were big and mirrored and perfect for hiding her face.

She turned to grin at Dylan when she noticed someone standing directly behind him. At first, he looked like just another traveler on his way to a plane. He wore a dark polo shirt and was putting his phone into his pocket. He pulled a small suitcase behind him.

He checked to make sure his phone was safe and looked up and directly at her. Recognition glowed in his eyes. She saw the scar on his cheek.

He had been at the fire. He knew who she was.

Their eyes met, and the man grinned. He pulled his phone back out, hit a button, and she could read his lips.

"I found her."

"Dylan," she whispered. She grabbed at his arm, forcing him to turn, but the man was already gone.

"What? What am I looking for?" Dylan asked. "Are you okay? You're shaking?"

"He was there," she whispered. "He was at the fire. I saw him."

Dylan's face went hard. He motioned to security, but Bonnie knew it was too late.

Security swarmed around her, but it didn't matter. The damage was already done.

They'd found her. They'd seen her with Dylan, and she knew a simple Google search would lead them right to Silver Springs. Dylan wasn't in hiding, so it would be easy enough to locate him. Hell, all they had to do was ask at Sandy's for him.

She suddenly regretted not being more careful. She should have taken more precautions. She should have stayed hidden.

"It'll be okay," Dylan told her, guiding her toward the plane. "Security is on it. You don't have to worry."

She let him take her onto the plane. She felt numb all over. She had hidden successfully for weeks now. If she had just walked to the plane without the stupid sunglasses, the man would have never seen her. They would have missed each other by seconds.

Instead, she had failed her brother.

She sat down in the soft leather chairs but didn't feel comfortable. She was clammy and hot and cold at the same time. Her stomach threatened to expel her breakfast.

They had found her.

Chapter 32

THE PLANE RIDE home was miserable. Bonnie alternated between terror and passive fear the entire flight home. She didn't have a plan. She wasn't sure what she was going to do now. She wasn't sure what the next steps were.

She needed to call Detective Patton. Dylan's security team never found the man with the scar at the airport, but she was sure she'd seen him. She was sure it wasn't just her imagination playing tricks on her. He'd seen her with Dylan.

It wouldn't be difficult to ask whose private jet was on runway three and then to do a simple Google search for the location of Dylan Abbott. It was common knowledge where he was working.

Dylan's car sped along the highway as they returned to the ranch. She stared out the window, not really seeing the mountains or the building storm.

In her mind's eye, she could see the Trio already

booking flights and renting big, black, scary SUVs with tinted windows that they could snatch her up off the street with. She could see them finding her at Sandy's and taking her and her hamburger back to New Jersey to silence her brother.

"Are you okay?" Dylan asked, putting his hand on her knee. She jumped sky high.

"I'm fine," she told him. She moved away from him in the small car. It was one of his nicer ones.

"Right," Dylan replied. He didn't sound convinced. "Do you want to come over to my place?"

"No," she said shortly.

Dylan sighed and pulled the car over to the side of the road. Bonnie immediately became agitated. She needed to get home.

"What are you doing?" she asked, glancing around. She was ready to get out and walk if necessary. It wasn't far. She could actually see her cabin from here. If she hurried, she could be on the road before dark.

"You're planning on running again, aren't you?" Dylan turned to her, his dark eyes watching her every movement.

Guilt tugged at her, but she pushed it away. She raised her chin. "Yes. It's not safe."

He sighed, hurt pulling his lips tight. "Bonnie, you promised me."

"I know," she said, hating how guilty she felt. "It's just that I can't put you, or the ranch, in danger. They'll be coming for me. I know it."

Thunder rumbled, echoing off the mountains. The ominous sound reflected through her entire being.

"Bonnie, I promised I'd keep you safe," he said, his voice gentle yet firm. "I'm going to keep that promise."

Beside them, two dark SUVs with pulled up. Dylan

waved them off before the security teams could interrupt their conversation. Two men with earpieces hopped out of the car and positioned themselves so that no one could sneak up on them.

"You don't understand," she whispered. Her mind went back to the fire. To the helpless feeling of watching her life burn. She remembered the police station. Brett had looked so small and afraid in the uncomfortable chairs. She didn't want her little brother to be scared anymore.

"I want to be with you, Bonnie."

She closed her eyes tighter, trying to fight back the tears. She could hear the gentle plunk of raindrops start to land on the windshield. The rainstorm was starting.

She'd arrived in a rainstorm, and now she was going to leave in one.

She reached for the door, her hand shaking as she gripped the handle. She didn't want to leave, but she was so afraid. Afraid for Dylan. Afraid for Tyson. Afraid for Brett.

Afraid for herself.

"Please don't leave," Dylan told her. His voice made her turn and look at him. His dark eyes were so sad. "Please. I love you."

Her fingers fumbled on the door handle. She didn't open it. Her heart was bursting. Joy, fear, sadness, relief, and love were all exploding out of her chest, and she wasn't sure what she was going to do with all of them.

"I love you, Bonnie," he repeated. His eyes were dark pools that drew her in. "Please don't leave."

She didn't go out in the rain. The rain came harder, making the car a cocoon for the two of them. The world outside was lost to the sound of rain and thunder. They were the only two humans left.

"I love you, too," she whispered.

"Then stay," he said, reaching for her cheek. His fingers were rough but gentle as she closed her eyes and leaned into his touch. "I promise to keep you safe."

With her eyes closed, she thought.

She loved him. She loved him more than she'd ever thought possible and the sheer amount of emotion she felt was terrifying. She let herself wonder if perhaps it wasn't part of her need to run. She was afraid he might break her heart. She was afraid she'd break his, and that was almost as bad.

She took a deep breath and opened her eyes.

Dylan was there. Just seeing him made her shoulders relax and her stomach stop twisting into knots. He loved her. He'd just said the words and the light in his eyes told her it was true.

"Okay," she whispered. She'd take this leap of faith. She'd stay and make a stand.

"Okay?" Dylan's eyebrows raised with hope.

"Okay," she told him. "I'll stay. I'm done running."

He leaned forward and kissed her. He kissed her like she'd just given him everything he'd ever wanted. He kissed her like she was the air he breathed.

Lightning flashed, and thunder rumbled, but they weren't in the storm. Together, they were safe. Together, they could survive any storm.

Chapter 33

BONNIE COULDN'T SIT STILL. She jumped at every sound. She saw shadows around every corner, and she heard every squeak, step, and breath of every person walking down the hall.

She was a mess.

Four days. Four days since they'd left New Orleans. She'd been jumping and living on little to no sleep for four days. Every time she closed her eyes, she saw the man with the scar on his cheek. He would grin and then lunge for her.

She'd wake up screaming and afraid to go back to sleep. Not even Dylan could get her to relax.

She'd called Detective Patton, but he said there was nothing he could do. They didn't have any reports coming into the station about the Trio. It was still business as usual. As far as the police knew, the Trio was still looking for her and didn't know where she was.

So, today, she sat outside watching the horses and trying to stay calm. She felt better by the horses. Anytime anyone approached, they would lift their heads to see who it was. They were better at spotting people than she was.

So far, they'd seen two kids, Laura, and a security guard. Nothing too dangerous there.

She sighed and put her head against the fence post. She was so tired. This was going to drive her insane. The waiting was the worst part. She knew the Trio saw her. She knew it was only a matter of time before they found her.

She considered running again, but she couldn't bring herself to even think of it. She didn't want to leave Dylan. She was going to ask him if they could take a trip though. Maybe he could show her the farm he grew up on. She'd love to meet his mom and sister. Plus, his farm was in the middle of nowhere, Kansas. She'd probably be safe there.

"Bonnie?"

Someone touched her shoulder, and she spun, defensively putting up her hands. She was ready to fight whoever just snuck up on her. She'd only had her eyes closed for a second, but somehow someone had snuck up on her.

"Bonnie? Are you okay?" Tyson asked, taking a step back. His big brown eyes had a little fear in them, and she immediately felt guilty. She glared at the horses. They were supposed to warn her about people coming up. The nearest one just flicked its ears and walked away.

"I'm so sorry, Tyson," she said, dropping low to be at his level. "You just startled me."

"I'm sorry, Bonnie." Tyson got smaller before her eyes.

"It's not your fault, Tyson," she told him. "I'm just feeling anxious today."

"Oh. Sometimes I get anxious about things, too," Tyson

said, a smile brightening his face. He gave her a big hug. "Hugs help."

Her heart melted into a puddle on the ground. This five-year-old was wise and kind. She hugged him hard back. "What were you coming to see me about?"

"I just wanted to see if we were going to have a swim lesson today. It's almost time."

"I would love to have the swim lesson," she told him. "I just lost track of time. How about we both go change and I'll meet you at the pool?"

She smiled and hoped he'd take her up on it. A swim lesson would help distract her.

Tyson nodded. "Okay."

"Come on," she said, rising up and putting a hand on his shoulder. "We can walk back together."

Tyson reached for her hand and held it tightly as they walked. She liked having the physical connection. He could always make her feel better. She sighed and looked around. The camp was quiet.

You're safe here, she reminded herself. She gave Tyson's hand a gentle squeeze, and he smiled up at her.

She didn't want to run, but she just wished she felt safe again.

TWO MORE DAYS PASSED. Bonnie sat on the back porch of the kitchen trying to eat her sandwich for lunch. It was almost a week since New Orleans, and still, there was nothing. She was starting to think that maybe she'd been seeing things. Maybe it wasn't the same man from the fire. Maybe it was just a man with a similar scar who she thought was him.

Detective Patton checked in with her daily, but he always said the same thing- no new leads. No new chatter.

The sandwich was one of Chef's best, but she couldn't find the desire to eat. She just kept picking off pieces of bread and chucking them off the deck. At least the squirrels and birds would get a good meal out of it.

Two security guards walked past, their uniforms dark in the afternoon sun. They both nodded politely in her direction, but they were all business. Since New Orleans, Dylan had the security teams doubled. No one was getting onto the ranch without them knowing.

She let her gaze wander to the garage. Dylan was under the hood of her car again. She sincerely suspected that he was replacing her entire engine. She shook her head. It was probably cheaper to just buy a new car, but he was having fun replacing and fixing up the junker. It tickled her that a billionaire was fixing up her car when he could buy her a new one six times over without even blinking.

Plus, he looked good with a little grease on him. He looked even better when he let her help shower it off.

"Hey, Bonnie?" Laura called, coming up to the porch. "Do you have a minute?"

"Sure. What do you need?" Bonnie set her sandwich off to the side.

"Can you help me with the kids?" Laura asked. "We've got extra kids coming in for the day, and I'm short staffed."

"I'd love to help," Bonnie told her. "Let me just put this in the kitchen."

"Oh, thank you! Just come to the barn. You're a life-saver!" Laura called, already walking toward the barn.

Bonnie headed into the kitchen, disposed of the sand-wich, and put her plate in the dishwasher. She liked having something to do, so she was happy to help Laura. Besides, she also liked working with the horses.

She jogged over to the barn where Laura had a line of kids finishing a horseback ride and a line of new kids getting ready to go. Laura pointed to the kids and mimed taking off her helmet, so that's what Bonnie did. She helped the kids take off their riding gear and then had them line up along the barn wall.

"Thank you so much," Laura told her, as she grabbed a riding helmet from Bonnie. "There's more kids than we expected today. A bunch of foster parents just brought all of their kids, so this really helps. Thanks."

"My pleasure," Bonnie assured her.

"If you can make sure all these kids get up to the cafeteria, Elena will make sure they get fed," Laura said. "I'm going to get this next group up and riding."

"Sounds good," she told Laura. She turned to the kids. "Okay, time for lunch!"

She wrangled the line of kids up the hill to the cafeteria where Elena had plates and food ready to go.

"I think I've got lunch handled," Elena told her. "Laura may need some more help, though."

"Sure, I'll head back to the barn," Bonnie replied with a smile. She felt better now that she was moving and doing something. She was sure Laura could use a hand with the kids, and then she could even help groom the horses. It was certainly something to do, and it felt better than being by herself.

She walked along the side of the barn. The sun was warm on her cheek, and she was glad she'd put sunscreen on that morning. She'd learned the hard way just how easy it was to burn up in the mountain altitude.

A noise made her pause. It sounded like a little kid

scuffing his feet against the barn doors. She shook her head. The camp kids had a bad habit of messing with the barn doors when they were bored. She was going to have to go put an end to that.

She turned the corner of the barn, fully prepared to yell at one of the kids to stop scuffing the paint, but there was no kid.

Instead, she suddenly had a bag over her head. The world faded away as she felt an arm wrap around her neck, choking the life out of her. The arm loosened a little, but she still felt herself losing consciousness. The world went dark as *they* took her.

Chapter 34

onnie

It was hot and hard to breathe. Her head hurt like hell.

Bonnie woke and struggled to remove the cloth from her face. She pulled at the dark fabric, finding that her hands were tied together in front of her and she was in a small enclosed space. She managed to get the pillowcase, or what she assumed was a pillowcase, off her head.

Then she had to work on not panicking.

Bonnie wasn't a fan of tight spaces. She wasn't exactly claustrophobic, but she didn't enjoy spelunking or being buried in a pillow fort. She liked being able to breathe and to stretch out without touching anything.

She couldn't do either of those things.

Panic clawed up from her stomach and gripped at her throat. She wanted to scream. She wanted to kick and thrash and fight for her freedom, but she knew that it wouldn't do any good. So, she closed her eyes, counted backward from ten and focused on her breathing.

It was an exercise she did with her autistic kids when they got overwhelmed. It worked. Her chest loosened and her heart beat more regularly the closer she got to one. Deep breathing also seemed to help the ache in her head.

You can do this, she told herself. She wasn't quite sure what "this" was just yet, but she was going to do her best not to freak out. She needed to stay calm and come up with a plan. Panic wasn't her friend right now.

"Three, two, one," she said softly. She took a deep breath and opened her eyes to evaluate what she could see.

She was in a small, dark space. It smelled faintly of gasoline. A pale glow caught her attention, and she wiggled to look at it. It was an emergency escape trunk light. She reached up and pulled at it, but nothing happened. She wasn't terribly surprised.

It was kind of stupid to lock someone in a trunk and keep the escape latch still working.

She'd heard that if someone ever kidnapped her and put her in the trunk of the car, that she should kick out the taillight. That way, anyone driving by them would see her, and the police would catch them.

She wiggled around in the tight space, very carefully ignoring just how tight it was, and tried to figure out where the taillights were. She guessed and kicked hard.

Nothing happened except it hurt her foot. She tried a different spot but heard a metal thud. Of course, if the kidnappers disabled the security latch, they would probably have a plan in place to protect the taillights too.

She sighed and tried to relax and think. There had to be something else she could do.

She wiggled, searching for her phone, but it wasn't in

her pocket. Her attacker probably took it. She did a mental inventory: shoes, jeans, t-shirt. Hands bound, hooded, and her head hurt like she'd been drugged. There wasn't a lot she could do with any of that.

She had seen on TV where a modern-day Sherlock Holmes was able to tell where in London they were by focusing on the sounds of the street and what direction the car was turning. She had no hope of doing that herself, but she figured she might at least keep her brain thinking.

The car wasn't on. The engine was running, but they weren't moving. She heard a voice coming from the front. She quieted her breathing and listened as hard as she could.

"No, Boss... Too much security... I don't... can't..." The words faded in and out, but only one voice said them. Whoever it was that had her was talking on the phone. The phone conversation continued with her kidnapper obviously getting frustrated. She wondered what had him staying stationary and why they weren't speeding down the mountain and calling her brother to keep him from testifying.

Her stomach twisted, not just from the stress, but from the pounding in her head. Whatever they'd used to knock her out was making her nauseous. She was just glad she hadn't eaten much of that sandwich. Given that she had no idea how long she'd been in the car, she didn't know how much of it she was going to throw up. At least there wasn't going to be much either way.

She closed her eyes to help her concentrate. Deep breaths, in and out. Go to your happy place. She'd guided so many kids into calmer spaces using this method. It was time she made it work for herself.

Go to your happy place.

She expected to find herself sitting on the beach in

Mexico sipping margaritas with her girlfriends, but that wasn't the memory she wanted. That didn't give her the peace she was looking for.

Instead, she wanted to be in the pool with Tyson and Dylan. She wanted to splash and hear their laughter. She imagined herself there in the pool with them. She could see Dylan's dark eyes smiling as he pretended to be a shark and chase Tyson. Tyson would shriek with delight, and he'd smile so wide it had to hurt.

That was her happy place. Those two were her happy place.

What if she never saw them again? What if they killed her to keep her brother from talking? The panic gripped at her throat, choking off her supply of air. She whimpered, unable to scream. She was afraid in a way she'd never thought possible. Every cell of her body shook with terror.

She heard the car door slam and the driver mumble something as he walked away. She had no idea what was happening or how to get out of this.

"Deep breaths, go to your happy place," she whispered. She thought of Tyson's sweet smile when he succeeded in swimming. She thought of the way Dylan's hand would rest on her hip as he stood beside her and watched their boy swim.

Slowly, she pushed the fear down and focused on them. They were who she was going to fight for. She was going to get back to them if it was the last thing she did.

Chapter 35

 *ylan*

DYLAN WAS WORRIED. He'd seen Bonnie walk to the barn, but then she didn't come back. He was waiting for her to come back so he could show her the updated car. He finally had it all fixed and ready for her. He'd basically put in a new engine, and he wanted to surprise her with it.

But he couldn't find her.

He called her phone and smiled when he heard her ringtone from inside the barn.

"There you are," he said, coming inside and looking in one of the horse stalls.

Except she wasn't there. He found her phone tucked in a saddlebag. It was only because the ringer was perpetually stuck on the loudest setting that he even found it.

Anxiety tumbled in his belly. There was something very wrong about this. Bonnie always had her phone. It was part of her escape plan if the Trio ever came here. She needed it. It was as much a part of her as her hand or her head.

Tension crept into his jaw.

He grabbed his phone and called security.

"This is Dylan Abbott. Bonnie Kincaid is missing," he announced as soon as the head of ranch security, Brian Cards, picked up.

"We have an issue at the West entrance," Brian told him. "We're locking the camp down. No one gets in or out. I'll spread the word that Bonnie is a priority."

"She's more than just a priority," Dylan growled.

"Of course, sir." Brian shouted an order to someone in the background before returning to the conversation. "I have four of my best men on it, and I'm running the security footage myself. I'm afraid that's all I can spare with what's going on at the West entrance."

"Find her." He shut off the phone angrily. There were few times in his life Dylan wished for old technology. Slamming the phone was one of them. There wasn't enough of a release angrily pushing the little red button. He wanted something to slam.

He stalked out of the barn. He wasn't sure quite where he was going, but he didn't want just to stand still and wait for security to find her. He felt the need to do something. He was never the kind to simply sit back and let others do for him, so he was going to go out and look for her.

He hoped he'd find her curled up under a tree with a good book. Maybe she was swimming or planning one of her sensory friendly activities in the kitchen.

The queasiness in his gut made him think that something bad had happened. There was an edginess and raw anxiety that he couldn't seem to shake, no matter how much he tried to come up with alternatives for where she could be.

He checked the area around the barn. He checked the hayloft. He walked out toward the horse pastures, but since the horses were all out on rides, he didn't go far. With every moment, he felt the dread deep in his bones increase.

Two security guards hurried past him as he walked away from the barn and back toward the garage. They spoke quickly into their radios and had determined, firm looks on their faces as they headed toward the West entrance. Something big had to be going on over there.

He paused, mid-step. Should he follow the security guards to the west? What if that's where Bonnie was and she needed help?

He shook his head. He'd just be in the way over there. He could only imagine the current chaos at the entrance. Today was pick-up and drop-off day. New kids were arriving while some stayed for another week. It meant that the parking area was always full of cars and kids. If there was an accident or a delay, it always turned into a disaster.

Instead, he decided to walk along the far path behind the garage. It was on the eastern edge of the property and usually quiet. Since the East entrance was gated off from the road, the only person he'd ever seen over here was Bonnie the night she'd arrived.

For some reason, it seemed like a good place to look.

He walked quietly and quickly. His eyes searched in the trees, and he saw one of the barn cats jump into a clump of grass and emerge a moment later with lunch. But no Bonnie.

There were lots of trees along the perimeter of the property. Long before Carter had purchased the place, someone had put a line of pine trees to act as a wind buffer. Tall evergreens stood against the pale blue of the summer sky. The smell of pine in the sunshine was strong. Every hundred yards or so, a couple of aspen trees managed to take hold and make a little grove of their own.

The sound of metal caught his attention. He slowed his steps and came around the tree line. Standing at the eastern gate was a man he didn't recognize. He was large and wore dark clothing that resembled the security teams.

He definitely looked dangerous enough to be on the security team, but Dylan didn't recognize him. He'd made a point of looking at all the photos of the security personnel that would be protecting Bonnie. He tried to remember if Brian had hired anyone new recently

The man swore and pulled at the chain holding the gate shut.

Why would security be trying to get out using the east entrance, he wondered. There wasn't a good reason. The gate was always locked. All staff and security knew that. There was no reason to open the gate.

Unless he wasn't security. Unless he was trying to get off the property while security was busy dealing with an issue on the west side.

Dylan searched the tree-line, his eyes looking for anything that was out of the ordinary. It took him a moment before he spotted the car tucked carefully into a grove of aspen and saplings. The dark green of the car hid well.

She was in that car. He didn't know how he knew it, just that he did. Bonnie was in that car.

He checked his phone. Would security get here in time?

He knew they wouldn't. It would only take the man at the gate a couple of minutes before he figured out how to unlock it. The process wasn't very hard. Dylan made a mental note to have Brian update that as soon as possible.

He sent a message to Brian to come to the east gate with as many men as possible. As he put his phone in his pocket, his fingers brushed the pocketknife he kept there. It wasn't much, but it was better than nothing. He pulled it out, keeping it loose in his hand.

Dylan crouched low and made his way over to the aspen grove. He moved through the dappled light, doing his best not to step on any branches or do anything that might give his position away. His breath was shallow, and he was sure the man would be able to hear his heartbeat.

Carefully, he moved to the driver's side door. The man at the gate swore again, and Dylan froze. The sound of the chains moving against the gate followed. Dylan didn't have much time. He had no doubt this would get ugly fast if the man caught him.

He cracked the door, staying low and trying to stay out of sight. The door opened with a low creak that made Dylan wince. He held his breath and looked out. The man hadn't noticed. He was too busy threading the chain from around the gate.

It was an older car, which Dylan was grateful for. It meant there was a trunk release, rather than having an electronic option that would be more difficult to get to. He pulled the lever and prayed the man didn't notice.

The trunk popped, but the man was too busy opening the gate. Dylan didn't have a second to spare. He pushed the door shut as quietly as possible and hurried back to the truck.

His heart was in his throat as he opened it. If she were hurt.. or worse... he didn't know what he'd do.

"Dylan?"

Her voice was rough as she sat up, blinking against the light.

He wanted to kiss her, to hold her, to tell her she was safe. But she wasn't safe. Not yet.

Dylan looked over at the gate to see it swing open. He grabbed Bonnie under the arms and pulled her out of the trunk, closing it hard. He hoped that the man was too distracted to notice the sound.

She clung to him, her breathing fast. He needed to hide her. There was a gooseberry bush growing near the back tire of the car. It wasn't big, but it was close. He carried her behind it and set her on the ground.

She looked up at him, and he put his finger to his lips. She nodded.

He couldn't fit behind the gooseberry bush. It simply wasn't big enough for the two of them. The sound of the man's footsteps as he returned from the gate filled his brain. Without thinking, he stabbed his pocketknife into the back tires and then ran behind one of the aspen trees.

He felt like a child playing hide and seek. All it would take was one look back to see a man hiding behind the slim tree. He got as low as he could, but all it would take was one good glance. He gripped the pocketknife in his hand and prayed.

If the man did see him, Dylan would use the pocketknife. He would make sure that the man saw Dylan and not Bonnie. He would keep her safe, even if it meant his life.

The man kicked at a stick, sending it flying into a tree. Dylan was sure his heartbeat was loud enough for the entire state to hear. The man paused as if listening.

Dylan took a slow deep breath. He was ready.

The man shrugged and opened the car door. The car groaned with the new weight as he slammed the door shut. The engine started, and the car rolled away.

Dylan didn't dare move until the car was past the gate.

Even then, he was afraid that the man would look back and see the two of them, hiding behind a tree and a bush. A three-year-old could find them if they looked.

But the car kept going. It pulled onto the dirt road, and the engine revved. A cloud of brown dust followed it as it escaped. He knew that his knife would give the driver a flat tire by the time he was down the mountain. The police would catch him easily.

"Dylan?" Bonnie's voice held panic and relief at the same time.

He ran to her.

She pressed her face into his shoulder as he held her to him, whispering his name like a mantra. He whispered hers right back. He held her to him, afraid that she might be ripped from his arms at any moment. He would never lose her again.

Chapter 36

onnie

THE NEXT WEEK was a blur of police officers, questions, security upgrades, and lawyers. Bonnie was overwhelmed by it all, especially after just being kidnapped and locked in a trunk.

But, through it all Dylan was there.

He was there when the security team found the two of them walking up to the house.

He was there when the police caught her kidnapper trying to get onto the highway with two flat tires.

He was there when she had to tell the police what happened and explain the bruises.

He held her hand when the lawyers came to explain what was happening next.

He promised her he would always be there.

And she believed him.

Every night, she slept in his bed. He was there when the

nightmares of being trapped in the trunk again would wake her. He would hold her and whisper calming words into her ear. He saved her every night, just as he had saved her from the trunk of that car.

A week after the incident, things finally seemed to settle back to normal. Well, as normal as things could be with the insane amount of security both Dylan and Carter hired for the ranch. She was set to testify at the trial for her kidnapper, and after what the Trio had done to stop her brother from testifying, Dylan wasn't taking any chances.

The police wanted to put her into hiding. Bonnie found it hilarious that *now*, after all of her running and telling the police the mob was out to get her, *now* they were going to do it. Except, she didn't want it now. Dylan was her protector. He was the one who would keep her safe. He'd already proven that he could.

Bonnie stared out the car window as Silver Springs vanished into the distance. Two unmarked black SUVs followed closely behind them. She saw them and ignored them, knowing she was safe.

Bonnie wasn't thinking about the police or the upcoming trial. Today, she was going swimming with her boys. Dylan and Bonnie were taking Tyson to a pool with water slides and a diving board. Dylan had rented the entire place out, so it would be just the three of them and Bonnie couldn't wait.

She sat in the car and bounced in her seat as Dylan drove them down into the city.

"I'm not sure who is more excited," Dylan said, turning of the highway and onto a smaller road. He glanced at his two passengers out of the corner of his eye. "Bonnie or Tyson?"

"I am!" Tyson announced from the back. He was bouncing up and down, too.

Bonnie laughed. For the first time in months, she wasn't afraid of going into the city. The mob had found her. The terrible thing she'd been running from for the past few months had happened. And she'd survived. She felt like she could take on the world.

"I don't know, Tyson," Bonnie said, turning around in her seat. "I'm pretty excited."

"I'm *super* excited," Tyson assured. He crossed his arms. "Super duper totally excited."

"That's pretty hard to beat," Dylan agreed. He pulled into an empty parking lot and both Bonnie and Tyson squealed with excitement.

The three rushed out of the car and went inside the building. It was the closest recreation center to Silver Springs, so it wasn't the fanciest or biggest, but it did have two water slides and a diving board.

Tyson grabbed Dylan and Bonnie's hands and pulled them past the front desk and toward the smell of chlorine. Bonnie grinned as they hurried to the pool and found an oasis of water park fun.

They left their clothes by the side of the pool. Tyson finished first and ran to the top of the nearest water slide. He didn't hesitate at the top. He just hopped on and took the slide down, not realizing the depth of the water below.

Bonnie held her breath as the boy who hated the feeling of water on his ears zoomed down the slide and dropped into the landing area. He was a good enough swimmer she wasn't worried about him drowning, but she was afraid of how he was going to react to the sudden sensation of water on his ears and face. She braced herself, ready for the sensory meltdown.

He came up, wiped his eyes, and grinned. "That was great!" he shouted. "Come do it with me, Bonnie!"

Bonnie stared at him, surprised and pleased. The water didn't scare him anymore. He had learned to overcome it and find the fun. He would never really enjoy being underwater, but he was no longer afraid of it. He no longer hated the sensation, and Bonnie couldn't have been prouder.

"I'll be right there," she told him. She watched as he got out of the pool and began the climb up the stairs to do it again.

Dylan kissed her cheek as he joined her at the pool's edge.

"What was that for?" she asked, turning to smile at him.

"No reason," he told her with a smile. "I just like to kiss you."

She grinned. "That's good, because I like to be kissed."

So, he kissed her again.

"Hurry up, guys!" Tyson called from the top of the waterslide stairs. "I'm going again! You can't beat me!"

With a whoop, he took off fearlessly down the slide.

"Do you think we can always be like this?" Bonnie asked Dylan as they watched the boy shriek with delight as he slid down.

"Wet and humid?" Dylan asked, motioning to the indoor pool. "Probably not unless we move here."

"No, you goof." Bonnie chuckled and bumped him with her hip. "I mean, the three of us. Happy and safe."

"Do you know anyone else needing to testify against the mob?" Dylan asked. "Any sisters running from the cartel?"

"Nope. Just me and my brother testifying against stone cold killers," she told him. "Tyson's an orphan, so as long as there aren't any crazy relatives, we're good there, too."

Dylan took her in his arms. His eyes held hers and kept her steady, even as her heart spun and danced. "Then yes."

"Really?" Joy bubbled up in Bonnie's chest.

"Really," Dylan replied. And he pressed his lips to hers, sealing the promise with a kiss.

Chapter 37

~Four months later~

BONNIE SMOOTHED the front of her skirt. There wasn't a wrinkle to be found on the soft gray fabric, but she smoothed it anyway. It helped calm her nerves.

"We're up," a lawyer told her. The man carried himself with such ease in the courthouse. He knew where to go, where to stand, how to dress. The lawyer knew the name of the security at the front entrance even. He was comfortable. Confident.

Bonnie was not.

"It'll be fine," Dylan whispered, taking her hand in his. He gave her a gentle squeeze. She nodded. She was afraid if she opened her mouth, she'd throw up. That would definitely be worse than a wrinkled skirt.

Dylan held her hand as they walked into the courtroom. She was glad he was there. She was glad that Dylan was with her for this. They'd started this as a couple. It was best they finished it as a couple.

The carpet was some sort of gray-green mixture. Two wooden tables sat before the judge. A stern looking woman looked out over her tall wooden bench at the two of them. She had strict eyes, and the state seal loomed over her like a watchful guardian.

Bonnie swallowed hard. She could do this.

She stood before the judge, Dylan beside her as Tyson was brought into the room.

As soon as he saw the two of them, his small face lit up with a bright smile.

Today was the day they were going to officially adopt him.

"This is Docket FA148-09. We'll start by swearing in your clients," the judge said. When she smiled, her whole demeanor changed. She was no longer intimidating, but she was excited. She was excited to help Dylan and Bonnie legally adopt Tyson. She was making a family.

The lawyer had prepped Bonnie. She would swear in and then answer a series of questions. Dylan would do the same. Today was supposed to be easier than the trial Brett had participated in. Bonnie had stayed far away from New Jersey while the Trio was on trial. They were all in jail now and no longer even considered a player in organized crime. Brett's testimony, as well as Bonnie's against the driver, had destroyed them.

She grinned as she looked at the judge. This time, she was excited to be in a courtroom.

"Do you swear to tell the whole truth and nothing but the truth?"

"Yes." Her voice was solid.

"State your name for the record, please," the judge requested.

"My name is Bonnie Abbott," she replied. She liked the way it sounded as it came off her tongue. She was still getting used to the new name, but it fit her well. She liked being Bonnie Abbott.

"Thank you, Mrs. Abbott," the lawyer told her. "I'm going to ask you some questions about the adoption. Is the child you are here to adopt named Tyson Moss?"

"Yes." She grinned at Tyson, and he grinned back. He looked so professional in his dress shirt and tie.

"Are you married to Mr. Dylan Abbott?" the lawyer asked.

"Yes." Dylan squeezed her hand and smiled.

It had been just a small ceremony at the ranch. She'd worn a simple white dress, and her parents had flown in from Europe. Brett was there, wearing his brand new police uniform. He'd joined the police academy once the murder trial was over. He was happy, and so was Bonnie.

"Do you have secure employment?" the lawyer asked.

"I do. I work at Mountain Hope Ranch as a teacher," she replied.

"And as you are married to Mr. Abbott, I'm sure you are financially stable," the judge responded with a chuckle.

"Do you have a place for you and the children to live?"

She grinned. "Yes."

It was in the town of Silver Springs, just up the road from the ranch. Dylan bought it for her as a wedding gift. It overlooked the city and had mountain views. Plus, there were three bedrooms for future children.

"Would you like to change the child's name?"

"Yes. We'd like to change his name to Tyson Abbott," she replied. That was a good name, too. She and Tyson were both Abbotts now. It felt right.

"Mr. Abbott, you will now answer the same questions," the lawyer announced.

Dylan sounded more confident than Bonnie did as he gave his answers. He couldn't stop smiling at her and Tyson as each question was asked.

"And now, Tyson." The lawyer smiled at the bubbly little boy bouncing up and down on the seat next to him. "Tyson, do you know why you are here today?"

"Yes. I'm here to be adopted!" He had a smile on his face from end-to-end.

The judge grinned at him.

"What does it mean to you to be adopted?" the lawyer asked.

"It means I get to have them be my real parents," Tyson replied. He wiggled in his seat with excitement. "It means we're a forever family."

"Do you want to be adopted by the Abbotts today and do you want your name to be changed?" the lawyer asked.

"Yes and yes." Tyson froze. "I mean, yes, *sir*."

The lawyer chuckled. "What's your name going to be?"

"Tyson Abbott." Tyson beamed as he said it. "I'm going to be Tyson Abbott."

"Okay, thank you, Tyson." The lawyer patted Tyson's shoulder. "I have no further questions, Your Honor."

The judge sifted through the paperwork on her desk.

"Okay, I have here a properly filed petition for the adoption of the child. Also based on the testimony and the report that I have from the Division of Youth and Family Services, which recommends the finalization of the adoption, I will enter a judgment of adoption today. This will establish the same relationship between the children and the adopting parents as if the child had been born to the adopting parents." The Judge set her paperwork to the side and beamed at the new family. "Congratulations."

Dylan hugged Tyson close to him, wrapping his arms around the boy and Bonnie. Bonnie's heart felt like it was going to burst with joy. She thought the joy she'd felt at her wedding was too great to bear. This was more. Every fiber of her being was beyond joyful.

They were a family.

Dylan kissed her cheek, and she held her two boys closer to her.

The love that they shared would go on forever. It was an endless kind of love.

His carefree life is enviable, his kisses are intoxicating, and she can almost imagine a life with him. But all vacations come to an end. And when Cassie invites him to visit her hometown, Wyatt reveals that he can never go back. Not to her town. Not to America. Not to civilization.

Cassie leaves, confused and heartbroken, wondering just who she got herself involved with. Suddenly, her predictable life gets turned upside down when she sees her picture splashed across the Internet. And when the tabloids come looking for the mature woman who found the lost billionaire, she has no idea what to do...

...until he comes back.

Escape With Me: A Midlife Love Story

ABOUT THE AUTHOR

New York Times and USA Today Bestseller Krista Lakes is a thirtysomething who recently rediscovered her passion for writing. She is living happily ever after with her Prince Charming. Her first kid just started preschool and she is happy to welcome her second child into her life, continuing her "Happily Ever After"!

Thank you for supporting an indie author. Anything you can do, whether it be writing a review, or even simply telling a fellow reader that you enjoyed this, helps me out immensely. Thanks!

Krista would love to hear from you! Please contact her at Krista.Lakes@gmail.com or friend her on Facebook!

Further reading:

Bad Boys and Babies
    Family Doctor's Baby
    The Billionaire's Baby Arrangement
    Crime Boss Baby

Kinds of Love
    A Forever Kind of Love
    A Wonderful Kind of Love
    An Endless Kind of Love

Billionaires and Brides

Yours Completely: A Cinderella Love Story

Yours Truly: A Cinderella Love Story

Yours Royally: A Cinderella Love Story

The "Kisses" series

Saltwater Kisses: A Billionaire Love Story

Kisses From Jack: The Other Side of Saltwater Kisses

Rainwater Kisses: A Billionaire Love Story

Champagne Kisses: A Timeless Love Story

Freshwater Kisses: A Billionaire Love Story

Sandcastle Kisses: A Billionaire Love Story

Hurricane Kisses: A Billionaire Love Story

Barefoot Kisses: A Billionaire Love Story

Sunrise Kisses: A Billionaire Love Story

Waterfall Kisses: A Billionaire Love Story

Island Kisses: A Billionaire Love Story

Other Novels

I Choose You: A Secret Billionaire Romance

His Every Desire: A Billionaire Seduction

Wolf Six's Salvation: A Shifter Love Story

Burned: A New Adult Love Story

Walking on Sunshine: A Sweet Summer Romance

An American Cinderella: A Royal Love Story

Mr. Darcy's Kiss: A Contemporary Pride and Prejudice

9 781948 467278